What A Woman Will Do . . .

The moment Cuchillo Oro saw Pete Green's head beginning to turn to inspect Marianna's bare breasts, the Apache made his move. His left hand went to the familiar hilt of the golden knife, drawing it in a whisper of sound in a frozen fraction of a second. He dove forward.

Green saw it coming out of the corner of his eye, but his reactions weren't fast enough. Marianna, all set to remove the rest of her clothing and let the fun begin, also saw the sudden flicker of movement and began to step back toward the stairs, a scream starting deep in her throat.

The tip of the golden knife opened up the deputy's wrist, slicing through the flesh and tendons like a razor. Green's gun dropped to the floor in a shower of blood, his fingers extending helplessly.

Cuchillo was a devastatingly effective fighting and killing force. He knew precisely what he was going to do even before he started to move, and everything went more or less according to plan. More or less . . .

The Apache Series:

by William M. James

Apache

#18

SLOW DYING

PINNACLE BOOKS   LOS ANGELES

APACHE #18: SLOW DYING

Copyright © 1980 by William M. James

An original Pinnacle Books edition, published for the first time anywhere.

First printing, November 1980

ISBN: 0-523-40695-9

Cover illustration by John Alvin

Printed in the United States of America

PINNACLE BOOKS, INC.
2029 Century Park East
Los Angeles, California 90067

This is for Liz—who has helped me find the road I'd never found. I loved her when I first saw her, and I'll love her until I die.

I am the enemy you killed, my friend.
Wilfred Owen, 1893–1918

Slow Dying

CHAPTER ONE

"Bring up the twelve-pounders!"

"All the mules are dead here, Sir!"

The mist blew about him, making the uniforms of the soldiers blur and shimmer like ghosts. There was clinging mud beneath his feet, forcing each step to be slow and painful. All around him there was a bedlam of screaming men and bursting shells, black-powder smoke adding to the sense of unreality. He could hardly make out whether the troops to his right and left were wearing uniforms of blue or gray.

"They're breakin' through on the ridge, Captain!" came a voice from his side, and he turned, but there was nobody there, the speaker having vanished in the murk.

His fingers gripped the slippery brass hilt of the saber, while his left hand held an empty pistol. His hat was gone, and he blinked, wiping away a thread of blood from his eyes with the torn sleeve of his jacket.

"Look at Jackson, Captain Mann!"

1

The piping voice was a young drummer boy, hefting a musket longer than he was, blood streaking his hands and arms, a cut across his shoulder. His eyes were wide with shock and fear.

"What?"

"There. See!"

Captain Thaddeus Mann stared through the fog that swirled around them and saw a group of men locked together in a desperate battle a half mile away across a steep-sided valley. The hill was dotted with corpses tangled together in death, but on the top stood a solitary figure surrounded with what looked like a rampart of rotting bodies, many of them little more than skeletons.

"I make him out," he replied.

"He holds the line!" screamed the boy, his voice trembling with emotion.

"Then hurrah for Jackson. See how he stands, like a wall of bones. Bones . . . " the officer replied, shaking his head at a sudden faintness.

There was the sound of silk rustling, and he looked behind him. A woman was walking past, oblivious to the bloody carnage about her, dressed in a long, flowing silk gown of the palest lilac. Her eyes were blue as the summer sky in Montana, and she smiled at Thaddeus Mann and then disappeared behind a small clump of trees.

"Rachel," he said, trying to take a step toward her, but his boots were clogged in the crimson mud, and he nearly fell. There was the whistling of an artillery shell, growing louder and louder, and he flinched away from it. The earth shook with the concussion of the explosion. He heard the screeching of metal fragments as they burst all around him, leaving him unscathed.

"Captain?" said the drummer boy at his side, in a questioning, conversational tone.

"Yes," Captain Mann replied as he turned to the boy. "Sweet blessed Jesus," he muttered.

The cannonball had taken the lad's right arm clean off at the shoulder as though he had been struck a blow by some giant cleaver. The severed limb lay at his feet, and as Mann looked down, he was horrified to see that the fingers were still curling and straightening with a hideous life of their own.

Blood jetted from the wound, dappling the ground around them like a fall shower. But to Captain Mann's dismay, the boy showed no sign that he was even aware of his injury. Though his face grew pale and he swayed a little on his feet, he still smiled gently at the officer.

"You know something, Captain?"

"In God's name, what, boy?"

"My father was an officer. He seduced my Ma, and she hanged herself when I was one year old."

"Then I am . . . ," but he could think of nothing more to say.

"Hanged herself in her garters, Captain. One fine Sunday morn."

With that it was as though someone had slashed through the strings that hold body and spirit together, and the boy slumped to the earth without another word, lying still and dead.

Thaddeus Mann turned and tried to run from the field of battle, dropping his gun and allowing the saber to slip from his fingers. His only wish was to flee this nightmare. He knew the fighting so well that it was almost as though the same scenes were being played over and over for him.

The fog cleared, and he was able to run once more, feeling dry earth beneath his boots. There was an avenue of tall and stately trees that helped to cut off the sounds of the battle behind him. Gradually, he slowed to a walk, holding his side where the running had pained him, feeling his breath grow less ragged.

The sun came out, diamond-bright and broken by the leaves of the trees. From among them Mann saw a beautiful white stallion that was moving slowly and picking at the lush grass at the edge of the forest. He smiled at it until it half turned, and he saw that it had been dreadfully wounded. A fragment of metal had ripped its flank and belly apart, and its intestines looped greasily about its rear hooves, trailing in the dust as it walked steadily toward him.

The officer began to run again, away from the double row of trees, toward a lake he could see glinting a half mile off. A raven swooped down from the warm air, its midnight wings brushing against his gray hair. Once more the Confederate officer eased his pace and gathered his breath. The long meadows had given way without his noticing it to cropped lawns, and there was a large white house visible behind a rambling bower of red roses. It was a colonnaded mansion like his own home in Georgia, but there was nobody to be seen anywhere. It was odd that there were no slaves working in the fields beyond the lake. They couldn't all have run

4

North to the comparative safety of the Union lines.

There was a polished table laid out with a spotless damask cloth covering it diagonally, set with silver cutlery and glittering crystal glasses. A decanter of red wine and a long vase with a single white rose were in the center. The wind had dropped, and Captain Mann stood still in a dome of total silence.

He was conscious that he was no longer alone, and he swung around to see a woman walking around the corner of the house, her arms held out toward him, almost pleadingly. She wore a white bonnet, which totally concealed her face from him, but he felt that he knew her.

"Rachel?" he whispered, unbelievingly. It couldn't be his wife, Rachel. He knew that she was dead, buried in the blazing ruins of Atlanta.

The silence was gone, and he could hear the noises of fighting coming closer. But he couldn't remember what battle it was. Antietam? Shiloh? Spotsylvania? Vicksburg? Or was it Chancellorsville? That was when Jackson had fallen; Mann remembered that.

The woman was coming nearer, almost running, her arms still outstretched to him. The sun was sinking lower behind her so that she was a black silhouette against a dazzling bowl of golden light. The Captain squinted, trying to make out the face under the brim of the white hat. A white hat decorated with red roses around the brim. His wife had worn a hat like that.

"Rachel?"

There was a crash behind him, and he saw that the table had fallen over, the glass and procelain had shattered. But there was no wind, and nobody was near it.

"Rachel?"

She was right by him, and he held his arms out to hold her. The hat fell back, held around her neck by ribbons, and he saw. . . .

"No . . . !"

It was a sigh, not a cry, that strangled in his throat at the charnel vision of horror. A blasphemous entity was in his arms. There was rank breath on his cheek from the yellowed stumps of teeth; shreds of withered skin decorated the bones of the skull; a few hanks of corn-yellow hair dangled from the scalp; red-rimmed sockets of wind-washed bone were where the eyes would have been.

Thaddeus Mann pushed away this gibbering specter of his wife and ran away from the great white house and the formal gardens, away from the lake and the trees and toward the fighting.

He hardly saw the soldier who was standing and waiting for him in the shadows, holding a .577 Enfield rifle musket with a bayonet fitted. The man wore dusty blue and had a half-smile on his lips as he saw the Reb officer running blindly toward him. He lowered the muzzle of the gun and braced himself for the impact.

Thaddeus Mann never saw the bayonet. He felt only a dull blow and the pain of something that grated between his ribs, bringing him toppling to the earth. His fingers scrabbled among the fallen leaves, and he felt his sight slipping away. But he could hear steps coming closer. The last he saw was a

6

woman in a long dress, wearing a white hat trimmed with red roses.

This time he screamed so loudly that he finally woke himself up.

CHAPTER TWO

Sheriff Thaddeus Mann, late captain in the Army of the Confederate States of America, had been the law in Pine's Peak since he had been demobilized from the infantry at the end of the fighting. He was a man at the far end of middle-age, with most of his past behind him and not a whole lot of future to look forward to.

Pine's Peak, in Colorado Territory, was a lot like its sheriff.

There'd been silver in what had looked like commercially viable quantities, and the mine had begun to thrive. The township had sprung up, and there'd been saloons and whorehouses, the beginnings of a church, a school and a half-dozen stores. But the great hope of Pine's Peak was the railroad.

The Kansas Pacific was opening up the center of the country, running across from St. Louis, through Kansas City, Fort Hays and Denver and up to Cheyenne, where it linked up with the Central Pacific to drive a path clear through to the Pacific at San Francisco. A committee of influential citizens had

9

been set up in Pine's Peak to arrange a contract for a spur line to join up with a new branch of the main railroad that they had heard was proposed to run in their direction. That had been back just after the War, around the time that Thaddeus Mann came to town.

Since then, a whole lot of things had gone wrong in the area. The information had been wrong. Simple as that. The Kansas Pacific had never intended to push out in the direction of Pine's Peak at all. So the settlement had built its spur for nothing. Seven miles of track started behind the optimistically named International Saloon and then stopped. Not anywhere in particular. Just stopped.

There were three trestle bridges and a high embankment as well as a short tunnel of about 60 feet hewn through living rock. The total cost was around 18,000 dollars more than the committee had anticipated, and the construction had resulted in 11 deaths from accidents and four from Indian attacks.

Then the silver lode began to fail. The quality of the ore deteriorated, and the quantity started to fall each month. Gradually, the town of Pine's Peak began to die, and Thaddeus Mann sat in his office and quietly watched it happen. It didn't worry him that much. His salary was paid, and it covered his expenses. On his arrival he'd been given a cabin on the edge of the town, and his needs were few and simple—basic food and three bottles of whiskey a week plus a visit to one of the two remaining brothels once every two weeks. He divided his favors equally between Jane's and Theresa's. The Harknett sisters had been in Pine's Peak since way back when, and they now kept their houses going with a fading supply of whores. Lately, they'd taken to using Indian girls and even a nigra bitch. But the town had drawn the line at that, and the black girl had been sent packing.

The only things that worried Mann were his dreams.

During the War he'd been an elderly captain, ready to retire from the Southern forces, but he'd stayed on throughout the hostilities. He'd seen action in most of the major battles and campaigns. Where younger men had given up and quietly put a ball through their heads, Thaddeus Mann had kept fighting. Despite his age and gray hair, he was one of the most experienced and toughest soldiers in the Army. He'd fought Indians for years, and then he'd taken part in bounty-hunting in Mexico. There wasn't a trick of killing or tracking or trapping that Mann didn't know.

If it hadn't been for his character, there was no doubt that he would have risen further and faster than a middle-aged captain. But Thaddeus Mann didn't much care. He didn't suffer fools gladly. Most times he didn't suffer them at all. And since, in his opinion, most of his superiors were fools, it's easy to see why he retired still a captain. And some said it was only his great skill that had saved him from demotion or even from a court-martial and a firing squad.

That insubordination had lasted with him in Pine's Peak, but the folks there recognized the steel that lay beneath the quiet exterior. Mann didn't hate anybody, but he kept the law. Didn't matter a flying

11

damn to him about justice or injustice. All that mattered was the law.

Thaddeus Mann had never been a light-hearted man. As a boy he'd studied hard with a view toward a military career, until family tragedies had sent him out into the world at the age of 13 to start earning a living with his fighting talents.

Only late in life did he glimpse the distant prospect of happiness when he met and loved and won Rachel Ashley, the wealthy daughter of a local cotton magnate. But the bitterness between the North and South had meant a short and wonderful marriage—a marriage that ended when his young bride was trapped in a blazing building and killed.

After that he didn't smile a whole lot.

In between the recurrent nightmares that haunted his sleeping hours, Thaddeus Mann was an excellent sheriff. But that was coming to an end. As the town died, the need for a top lawman slipped away, and he knew that the time couldn't be that far off when they would ask him to quit. Then he'd live for a while in peace in the little house, and after that . . . After that he'd maybe move away west and see the Pacific one last time.

Things weren't so good. He could no longer pick and choose his deputies, and he was left with a mixture of passing drifters and local sweepings. Most were young boys in their early 20s or late teens who were eager for trouble when drunk, and just ordinary mean when they were sober. Boys that he would never have looked at in the old days, but now it was them or nothing. And with occasional outbursts of fighting with the local Indians, they were just a mite better than nothing.

"What the hell happens if bigger trouble comes along?" he asked nobody in particular as he looked out of the window at the early morning.

Four miles away, in a shelter beneath an overhanging rock, something better in the way of trouble was also awake, standing and stretching the night's chill out of his bones, feeling the muscles crack as he extended them to the limit.

He was big even by the standards of white men. But he was an Apache, a member of the Mimbrenos tribe. Six feet tall and broadly built, his only physical imperfection was a mutilated right hand where a Cavalry officer named Cyrus Pinner had tortured him. It had taken him years, but the Apache had finally tracked Pinner down and killed him.

He drew a knife from its buckskin sheath at his right hip. The dawn sun flashed off the polished blade and the uncut stones in the rough, golden hilt. It was the knife that had given the Apache a name that made him notorious throughout the southern and western regions of America.

Golden Knife. Cuchillo Oro!

CHAPTER THREE

For a long time after the end of the Civil War, there wasn't a whole lot of trouble with the Indians in that part of the Colorado Territory. The local Utes were mostly peaceable, and the Cheyenne and Arapaho to the north and east of Pine's Peak had also been quiet; though occasionally there'd be a few young bucks who'd break out and go raiding, trying to re-kindle the dying ashes of their people's pride.

It was that same racial shame that also brought the old men to the settlement—warriors who remembered the great days of fighting the white set-tlers and the pony soldiers of the Cavalry. They would sit cross-legged by the smouldering campfires and tell of the herds of buffalo and of the vast rivers of living creatures that a man might stand and watch for a day and never see the beginning or the end.

But that was over.

Wounded Bear and Crooked Eye were two of the oldest men in the local Ute tribe. Wounded Bear was in his 50th summer. He had a beer gut that toppled him forward if he tried to run and a necklace that he told the whites was made from the bones of animals he had killed when a young warrior. But the other men of his tribe knew that they were, in truth, the knuckle bones of six of the yellow-stripe soldiers that he had personally killed. Crooked Eye was a little taller than his old friend and a year or so younger. But he had suffered grievously in a fight against the whites nearly 20 years back, and an empty eye socket told its own tale, as did the scars that seamed his body and the turned ankle that forced him to walk at a slow, limping pace.

They had known each other all their lives, from being bare-butted boys scrabbling in the dust to being brave warriors, full of fiery life and courage, each taking a girl to be his wife and raising a brood of fine children. But the summers and winters had come and gone in the high Colorado country, and the white men had eaten away at their hunting grounds—soldiers and miners and then towns. The old ways died swiftly, and many of the Utes died with them. Unscrupulous Indian agents brought in wagons of blankets infected with smallpox and even with cholera. Diseases spread through the huddled camps with the speed of a prairie fire. Their squaws and most of their children had died. And in the end there were the two old men, one partially blind and limping, the other too fat to run, linked together by the hosts of their memories.

Every Friday afternoon they would go together from their camp, both on sway-backed mules, and come into Pine's Peak. There'd been a time, years back, when the town wouldn't tolerate any Indians or blacks in any shop or saloon. But decreased trade is a wonderful cure for racial inequality, and the barriers came down as the township grew more poor. Even two drunk old Utes, like Wounded Bear and Crooked Eye, were better than nothing to the owner of the International.

They both bought themselves whiskey and sat quietly in a corner of the empty room. Crooked Eye had been lucky enough to find a pistol outside of town the day before with its owner's name engraved on the butt. There was one young church-educated half-breed in the area, and he had told the old man where to take the gun. It had belonged to an ex-soldier named Quincannon, who had given the Ute three dollars as a reward for returning his treasured pistol. Crooked Eye and Wounded Bear were determined to drink that money away in the shortest possible time.

It was fine until late afternoon. Sheriff Mann had ridden out to talk to some homesteaders about the water rights, and the deputies were in charge of Pine's Peak. There were four of thém, all roughly the same age and all of them local boys.

There were the Green twins, Pete and Sheldon. If you put their brains together, you'd finish up with the intelligence of a fence post. Twenty-one years old, the Greens were only mean when they were bored, but they started getting bored when they woke around 11 o'clock in the morning, and they generally stayed that way until they dropped back into their unmade beds somewhere after midnight.

The youngest of the deputies was Albie Chesterman, who was just 18. Albie was around 6' 9" tall, and folks in Pine's Peak said that he was so skinny he had to run around in a rainstorm if he wanted to get wet. But they only whispered it behind his back. Albie had very little sense of humor, though setting fire to stray dogs could make him laugh for hours. And he also had a hair-trigger temper, which made any attempt at a joke dangerous in the extreme.

The fourth upholder of law and order was Larry Feathers. Tall and good-looking, he was the scourge of the ladies in the town, and he had a way with angry boyfriends and husbands that was very persuasive. When you'd been persuaded by Larry, you stayed persuaded—sometimes forever. Larry was a big, strong, broad-built lad of 20. He was nicknamed "Hoss" by his friends; the rest of Pine's Peak called him a mean-minded, horny, son-of-a-bitch bastard.

None of the deputies liked Indians very much, which was why the late afternoon saw Wounded Bear in the cell, hands manacled behind him, nose broken and bleeding, with Crooked Eye moaning, lying on the dirt floor of the same cell, nursing a broken wrist and missing most of his remaining teeth.

It hadn't taken a lot of doing to get themselves into that state. Wounded Bear and Crooked Eye were simply two, old drunk Utes sitting right behind a running flush, leaning on a table in the corner of a saloon in Pine's Peak. And it was the butt end of a hot and boring day for Albie, Pete, Hoss and Sheldon.

It was an unbeatable combination.

* * *

The only deputy that Thaddeus Mann had any time for was a man even older than himself. Dave Tardy had been in his late 40s way back in the spring of 1850 when he was one of 50,000 hopeful prospectors who poured through Fort Laramie on their way to the rich goldfields of California and Oregon. Tardy had spent a whole lot of time grubbing in the bottoms of shadowed canyons, and precious little tasting the clean air up on the tops and pinnacles of the mountains.

He'd lost a leg when an ox wagon had overturned on a muddy gradient one bitter November afternoon, and only a traveling quack had saved his life. Then he'd drifted, using his skill with guns to keep him alive. There'd been a time when Dave Tardy had earned his keep by firing guns for bounties. Now he just repaired them.

Thaddeus Mann hadn't been in Pine's Peak long when Tardy drifted in on a chestnut mare that had a strange, skittering gait to her, like she was going up a ladder. The two men had taken an instinctive liking to each other, and Tardy had finally accepted the job of first deputy to the sheriff, with special responsibility for taking care of the office and the jail, as well as guarding the prisoners. In bad times he'd come hobbling out—once using an upturned broom when he couldn't lay his hands on his crutches—and had blasted a trio of bank robbers clean off their horses with a heavy-gauge Meteor scattergun.

Dave Tardy disliked the four boys even more than Mann did, and he was annoyed when they came whooping in, kicking mud all across his scrubbed floor, dragging Wounded Bear and Crooked Eye after them like a couple of bloodied sides of meat.

Though he moaned under his breath at them, Tardy knew better than to try and face up to them. Not one of the four was worth a plugged nickel to his way of thinking, but that didn't stop him from being scared of their mean, vicious natures. So he'd unlocked the doors of the cell and stood back while they booted the two Indians inside, stringing Wounded Bear up to the bars and kicking him savagely in the groin so that he retched and fought for breath. Then Tardy locked up again and sat back down in the worn chair behind the desk. He heard the four boys yelping their way across the street to the saloon to celebrate their latest arrests.

When he tried to roll himself a cigarette, Tardy was surprised to find out how much his fingers were trembling.

It was coming on toward evening.

Cuchillo Oro glanced up at the western sky and saw how the setting sun was already scraping at the tops of the mountains. There was a small town near here, he remembered, though it had been many years since he had last walked that way. Then they had been building a railway, he recalled, with rails that had begun just behind one of their many saloons. Cuchillo had always been fond of liquor; it was a weakness that he still tried hard to keep under control. He had a few dollars in the small leather bag at his waist, and he licked his lips at the idea of some good American whiskey. It would warm his belly and help him hold the memories at bay.

Still they plagued him, much as they plagued the lawman that he had never met. Cuchillo also recalled a dead wife and a child too. Both were murdered by Cyrus Pinner, the Cavalry soldier whose vendetta against the big Apache had made them the talk of the Southwest for years. "Pinner's Indian" they had called Cuchillo Oro, and it had been a name that he had hated. Now Pinner was dead, his drowned corpse washed away to hell, with the livid marks of Cuchillo's fingers tight around its throat.

The last year or so Cuchillo hadn't heard the phrase "Pinner's Indian" so much.

Finally, he rounded the bend in the trail that revealed the township to his keen eyes. It was smaller than he remembered it, but he had found, as he grew from adolescence into manhood, that this was often the case. The remembered slopes were less steep, and the rivers not so wide. The chiefs seemed shrunken against the loud-voiced heroes of his youth, and the colds and heats were less extreme.

"Cuchillo says that one thing does not change," he muttered to himself. "The white man is still never to be trusted."

The arguments over the water rights had been longer and more bitter than Thaddeus Mann had expected, lasting well past noon and dragging acrimoniously on into the afternoon. At last it had been necessary for him to raise his voice to the two wrangling farmers and allow his hand to drop easily to the butt of his trusted Navy Colt. Both men had

21

known the sheriff long enough to be aware that when his tones grew louder and the fingers reached for the .36 that it was time to settle the argument and let his temper cool.

Mann clicked his tongue to the mare that pulled the light rig that carried him around when he was on official business, but he wasn't in too much of a hurry. There might be time for a steak and some eggs before he looked in on Dave Tardy. "Only a half mile, old girl," he said, letting a thin smile hang around his lips for a moment as the horse pricked up her ears and raised her pace to a fast trot. She knew well enough that they were nearly home.

Cuchillo heard the sound of the wheels and the horse's hooves some time before he actually saw Sheriff Mann coming up behind him. He made no effort to get clear of the trail. There wasn't any reason for him to do that. He wasn't a wanted man anywhere in the country. No lawman had flyers out on him; so he could come and go where and when he pleased. But Cuchillo had experienced enough trouble in his short life to know that the ways of the white men were not always the ways of the lawbooks.

So he eased the great golden knife in its sheath and moved to one side, looking back to see what was coming after him. There were times when the lone Apache wished that he carried a handgun, but he had never liked pistols nor rifles, though he was a better-than-average shot with either weapon. After Pinner had hacked at his right hand, Cuchillo had gone alone into the desert wilderness and spent

22

painful weeks in teaching himself to fight and shoot with his left hand. With a rifle, that wasn't too difficult, but the quick and efficient use of a pistol was much harder, and he still sometimes fumbled the action when he most needed speed and accuracy.

At last the rig appeared, and he saw that it held a single rider—a bare-headed elderly man, looking from the gray hair to be close to 60. He sat up high and erect on the seat. As soon as Thaddeus Mann saw the tall Apache standing there, he eased in on the reins and made sure the retaining thong over the hammer of the Navy Colt was free for a fast draw. He instinctively raked the hills and scrub around him for any sign of life, wondering if this was some kind of a trap. It would have been easy to have killed him, however, without the need for any kind of human bait.

Cuchillo stood still, making sure that his hands were clearly out of view. The white man finally pulled in to a stop about 15 paces away. Then he reached up slowly and eased back the front of his dark-blue jacket to show the Indian the polished silver star pinned to the left side of his vest.

"You alone?" asked Mann.

"Yes."

"Got a name? Seems you're a ways off your hunting grounds for an Apache."

"We are traveling people, the Mimbrenos."

"Didn't catch the name I asked for, Mister."

"You are the sheriff of this town?"

"Yeah. Name's Thaddeus Mann. Peace officer of Pine's Peak yonder. You carryin' a gun?"

Cuchillo held his arms wide and turned slowly

23

around so that the white man could see he was not armed. The setting sun bounced off the hilt of the knife in a burst of deep colors. Mann saw it and blinked.

"I was goin' to ask your name for the third time, Indian. Not a thing I like doin', but I figure you just spared me the trouble."

"I do not know you, Sheriff Mann," said the Apache, quietly.

"But I know you, Cuchillo Oro. That's the name, isn't it? And that's the golden knife at your belt there. The one there was so much killin' over."

"That is true."

Mann laughed. A sudden, sharp, barking sound. "Hell! Doesn't take a lot of brains to add up some facts." He held the reins in his left hand and ticked off points on his fingers. "Big Apache . . . on his own. Biggest Indian I ever saw, 'ceptin' old Red Shirt."

"Mangas Colorado was my grandfather," said Cuchillo.

"Heard that. Yeah. Mimbrenos. Damned stiff-backed lookin' buck at that. And the gold knife the ace kicker you need."

"I am not wanted for any crime," the Apache replied, standing balanced on the balls of his feet, ready for violent action if the white man made a move against him.

"No. You passin' through?"

"Yes. I wish to stay the night in . . . Pine's Peak, it is called?"

"That's what it's called. But I figure you aren't staying there, son."

24

"Why not?"

"Because I'm goin' to ask you nice and friendly to take that trail yonder, to the left."

"Why?"

"It passes the town, son, and brings you out clean the other side, near where the railroad line cuts across the river."

Cuchillo nodded his understanding. "Though I am not a criminal or a maker of trouble, you will still not allow me to stay even for one night?"

Mann nodded. "That's 'bout the left and right of it, Cuchillo Oro."

The Apache could feel his temper beginning to rise, and his left hand crept toward the hilt of the knife. "Then you do not keep the law. That is wrong!"

The sheriff saw the threat and drew his pistol in an easy, fluid movement and pointed it toward Cuchillo. "Keep the fingers off that blade, boy. Be the biggest mistake you ever made."

"You break the law!"

"Don't you ever say that to me, Indian. I live by the law!" He hesitated a moment. "You damned near made me lose my temper."

"By what right then do you threaten me with your gun and run me from this place?"

"Might be truth, what you say 'bout not being any wanteds out against you. But you're trouble, Cuchillo Oro. Where your feet land, men die. I'm not havin' that in my town. So you climb up here, slow and easy, and I'll even drive you out that far side."

* * *

25

There was no conversation. With the lawman driving the light wagon, it would have been easy for Cuchillo to have attacked him and knocked him to the ground. Both of them knew that, and both of them knew that the Apache wasn't really going to try anything. It wasn't worth it. Thaddeus Mann hadn't even bothered to take the knife away from him, though he was curious to see the legendary, triangular-bladed cinqueda.

They went along by the railroad. The metal was rusting and the ties were rotting in the years of neglect. The sheriff seemed like he was going to say something and then changed his mind and kept silent. He finally spoke when they reached the bridge on the far side of Pine's Peak.

"Get on down, Cuchillo Oro."

"You know that this is not right, and you still make me do it."

"Sure. Like they say about a man havin' to do what he has to do. This way, it's for the best, and nobody goes and gets himself hurt—even killed. Haven't had a murder in a while. Not anyone from outside."

"If I say that I will not go . . . ?"

Mann grinned at him. "Then you get pulled in as a vagrant, Cuchillo Oro. I got some mean little bastards as deputies, and they don't take to Indians. Specially they wouldn't take to a church-taught boy like you."

"Not church."

He had been taught by the little white man, John Hedges, who was perhaps the only good person of that race the tall Apache had ever met. But it had

26

been long since he had seen the ex-teacher. Perhaps Hedges was dead.

"Don't signify," said the sheriff, interrupting his train of memories. "Down and away, boy. I'll be back out this way in a half hour, and I don't look to see you anywheres around."

Cuchillo didn't answer. He climbed off the rig and stood still by the side of the road, watching as the lawman whipped up his horse and rattled away, back toward the town.

He didn't move, and his impassive face betrayed none of the anger that he was feeling for being treated like a rabid animal—just because of his race.

Sheriff Thaddeus Mann looked in at the jail, shaking his head at the sight of the battered faces and bodies of the two old Indians. But he knew the Utes would never dare to make a complaint against the deputies. So he left them in charge, ready to go on home. But an impulse made him head out toward where he'd left Cuchillo Oro. There'd been something about the attitude of the Apache warrior that nagged at him.

Cuchillo was still there. Unmoving, watching the lawman head toward him.

Twenty minutes later he was being locked up in the same cell as the Utes, charged with ignoring a town ordinance and vagrancy.

CHAPTER FOUR

Pine's Peak wasn't the worst jail that Cuchillo had ever been in. When he sat down and thought about it, he had to admit that it was one of the best.

The walls were solid and dry, and the ceiling didn't show any signs of leaking. There'd been a prison once, down in Baja California, where tidal waters ran clean through the cells. So each time the Pacific came sweeping through the inlet where the jail stood, it cleansed away all the rubbish and filth that might otherwise have accumulated and bred infection. There was one problem for the prisoners though. Unless they clambered up the bars of the door and hung there like ragged monkeys, they drowned. Cuchillo nodded to himself at the memory; that had probably been the worst he'd been in.

When Thaddeus Mann marched the Apache in, past four sniggering young men wearing deputies' badges, there were already a couple of battered Utes. They were old men, both well past middle age. One was manacled to the bars, and the other lay on the floor, barely conscious. Neither of them showed any sign of interest when the young warrior joined them.

"I'm a man of my word, Indian," said Mann. "You surely would have done well to have gone on your way, quiet."

"I will not do what I know is wrong," replied Cuchillo Oro as he sat down on the single bed in the corner of the cell.

"Boy!" exclaimed Albie Chesterman. "But he is a real smart-ass, ain't he?"

"Hate a smart-ass Indian," added Sheldon Green, spitting through the heavy bars, nearly hitting Crooked Eye.

"Worse than an uppity nigra," threw in his twin brother, Pete, for good measure.

Larry Feathers didn't say anything. He just came over and stared at the Apache, his handsome face totally without expression.

Cuchillo looked back at them, recognizing the type. Small-town mean. Boys with nothing to do but drink and fuck around and get meaner and meaner. He was already beginning to have some second thoughts about taking a stand against Sheriff Thaddeus Mann now that he saw the dogs that ran at his heels.

The sheriff went on home after a few minutes, leaving his deputies busily demolishing their second bottle of liquor. Their faces were becoming flushed, and their voices louder. Cuchillo recognized the danger signs from previous encounters with drunk whites, and he curled up on the bunk, trying to keep himself out of trouble. But beneath the appearance of dozing, his body was coiled and tense, ready for the attack.

The main door opened, and in came an elderly man who was hobbling on crutches and struggling with a tray of sandwiches. The four boys started to jeer at him for being a clumsy cripple, but Dave Tardy took no notice of them, laying the crutches against the desk and lowering himself into a chair.

"Gettin' colder than a witch's tits out there," he said.

"Could do with some warm tits tonight," grinned one of the boys. In the hour or so he'd been in the jail, Cuchillo had already worked out their names by listening to their banter. There was nothing else to do, locked away. The Utes had ignored him. Well, that wasn't totally true. The one on the floor didn't seem to have come around yet; he was lying still, eyes closed, blood crusting on his face. The one chained to the bars had looked across at the young Apache, but said nothing, his beaten face showing no expression.

"Should get that cock of your'n round to Teresa's place," replied Pete Green.

Larry Feathers took the banter as his due, spreading his shoulders under the tight shirt, smirking as he touched himself in the groin.

"Guess I got somethin' down here that them bitches'd weep for."

"If you have the money, son," said the old man.

"You, Dave Tardy," said the one called Chesterman, his voice slow and cold, "would do well to lock that flappin' lip. Day'll come and the sheriff ain't goin' to be around."

31

Tardy didn't blink. He rolled himself a cigarette, running a leathery tongue along the paper. "Be round long after you get to lay in the dirt, lookin' up at the sun with your eyes goin' blind."

"By God, but if I get the job of lawman here, then you'll not even get ten cents for shovelin' horseshit from an empty corral," snapped Albie, uncoiling his 6' 9" frame and looming menacingly over the cripple.

"Leave him be, Albie," called Pete Green.

"He's a bastard."

"He don't mean a fuckin' thing."

"I'll break his other God-damned leg for him and ram it clean up his ass!"

Tardy chuckled at the threat, puffing smoke past the boy. Green carried on, trying to spread a little oil on the bitterly troubled waters.

"Shut up, Dave. Let it alone."

"I mean it, Pete," said the skinny teenager, one hand hovering around his right hip where he kept a Peacemaker tied fashionably low. Too low, Cuchillo Oro had considered, figuring that the boy would have to reach down that extra inch or so too far if he came up against a really top gun—someone like Jed Herne or that ex-cavalryman that the Apache had been hearing a lot about recently. Crow, he was called.

"He'll keep quiet," said Green. "Won't you, Dave?" He interpreted the silence as agreement. "There. Honestly, Albie. Sincerely, I mean it. Trust me."

"I trust you, brother," said Sheldon Green, "just round 'bout as far as I can spit raccoon crap."

32

There was a brief silence in the jailhouse, and Larry Feathers walked over and stared closely at the prisoner shackled to the cell wall.

"Guess we'll let him down for the night."

"No. Leave the old buzzard," said Albie Chesterman.

"What have they done?" asked Cuchillo Oro, unable to hold back his curiosity.

"Mister Mann says how you're somethin' real special for a stinkin' Indian," replied Pete Green, who stopped picking his nose and stared at the golden knife that lay on the sheriff's desk where he'd thrown it. All of them had looked at it, each boy wishing that it was his. But Mann's word still ran, and none of them would have dared steal it.

"Yeah. Killed lots of soldiers, didn'ya? Not that it bothers us. Few blue-bellies here or there don't give a whistlin' shit to us."

There was a murmur of agreement from the rest of them, except for Dave Tardy, who sat quietly smoking. He shifted as his severed leg pained him, like it always did when the weather was going to change. Some cold mornings he would swear he could feel cold in the toes he'd lost so long back. The cell keys at his belt jangled with his movement, tinkling like the bells on a far-off sleigh.

"I did not hear your answer to my question about these Utes. They are old men."

"Sure are," agreed Larry Feathers. "Not like you. Surely are a big bastard, ain't he? Must be close to my height."

"The answer?" repeated Cuchillo, patiently. "I do not hear it." He wished that he hadn't begun to ask, sensing that this could be the moment they would all come piling in the cell after him. They'd beat him to the floor and then go to work on him with their boots, snapping ribs and battering him unconscious so that he could no longer roll and try and protect his groin and face.

Then he would die.

It could have been the moment, but it passed. The good old boys hadn't drunk enough to make them sufficiently killing mean. And, the truth was, all of them were just a touch scared of the big Indian. None of them wanted to be first in through that barred door—except for Albie Chesterman, who had no fear of anything, no sense of humor and no love for anything or anyone.

So they stayed where they were and talked to Cuchillo. They told him about Crooked Eye and Wounded Bear, the trouble they had with drunk Indians. They talked about how Sheriff Mann was too damned soft and how they preferred to deal with trouble-making nigras and Indians and Mexes and chinks themselves.

"Some of them gets accidents," laughed Feathers.

"Sure, Hoss. They fall down the steps in the jail-house here," said one of the twins.

Cuchillo was puzzled for a moment, thinking that he had not properly understood Sheldon's comment. He wondered why it caused such choking mirth.

"There are no stairs here."

"That's it, 'pache. Got it first shot. You sure are one clever mission-taught Indian, ain't you. Yeah, got it first damned shot."

Finally, as time wore on, their beds became attractive to them. Dave Tardy raised himself quietly from his chair and unlocked the manacles on the wrists of the old Ute, allowing him to slump to his knees. The young boys turned and watched curiously, saying nothing, then they returned to their drinking and cards. The warrior on the floor blinked himself back to the world, and the two old Indians crawled and sat close together in the corner of the cell farthest away from Cuchillo.

The Apache was feeling tired. He had a sick feeling at the pit of his stomach that the whites would not allow him free of their township without exacting some kind of a toll from him—toll that would be paid for with blood and bones and, possibly, with his life. What was one Indian more or less to them?

He loosened the long scarf of patterned cotton from around his forehead and let it lie on his lap. He fumbled in his breeches' pocket as he rolled half on his side to get more comfortable. There were three or four small coins in there that the sheriff hadn't bothered to remove. Cuchillo took them out and began to roll them in his fingers, placing them on his headband and then moving them again.

It was all some kind of a game designed to pass the time.

It was around midnight when the deputies left, kicking their chairs over and breaking the bottles into a can at the corner of the office. They muttered goodnights to Dave Tardy, but the old man studiously ignored them. They slammed the outer door behind them, finally leaving the building in silence. After around five minutes the last of the town's lawmen shifted and craned around in his chair, looking at the three prisoners.

"Any of you want anything? Can't offer you a four-course meal, but we got bread and some biscuits. There's some salt pork out back. Water?" None of them answered him. The Utes were locked in their own misery.

Cuchillo finally looked up at the white man. "I want nothing, but I thank you."

"Speak good English, Indian. Sorry to see you locked up here with that rubbish."

"That rubbish has been made by your people," replied Cuchillo. "Once they were whole men; now they are not. It has been the whites that have butchered and taken women and robbed my people."

Tardy shook his head. "Guess there's something in that. Thaddeus Mann and me ain't really whole. Couple of old desperadoes waiting for that last train to the depot, that's us."

"How did you lose the leg?" Cuchillo was interested in the old-timer, sensing that he lacked the bitterness and hostility of the four boys. But the Apache still would not trust any white man—or woman.

"Ox wagon. Rolled on me in mud on a steep grade. Sheriff's crippled too."

"I did not see it."

Tardy croaked his laughter and reached for his crutch. He stood up and hobbled clumsily nearer to the bars. "Some scars you see. Some you don't. Thaddeus had a bad time in the War. Lost loved ones. You know?"

Cuchillo nodded. "Yes. I know of losing loved

ones." His mind slipped back through time and space to his wife and baby, who were slaughtered years past by Cyrus Pinner. But the pig-faced pony-soldier had also gone that long road to follow them.

"Sure I can't do somethin' for you? Or some water to clean up those boys? Not that there's a lot of point in botherin' with that. Hoss, Albie and the twins'll be back on the morrow for some more funnin' with them."

"Funning?"

"They call it. What you see there ain't nothin', son." Tardy pointed through the bars at Wounded Bear and Crooked Eye, both liberally slobbered with dried and drying blood.

"They will beat them?" asked Cuchillo, who rose slowly from his bunk and took a couple of steps toward the friendly old cripple.

"Sure as sun comes up over thither and sinks hither. Beat the crap out of 'em. And as for you, they'll . . ." Then he stopped, knowing he'd crossed a line he shouldn't have gone over. He turned away again. The keys jingled once more at the broad leather belt.

One of the Utes muttered something to Cuchillo, but it was said low, and he wasn't that familiar with their tongue. But he caught the word "hang." And that was about all he needed to hear.

"I have broken no law."

"Sheriff told you to move on, boy. Kind of foolish of you not to do that. Thaddeus does things by his lawbook, or he don't do 'em at all. Ain't many times he don't do 'em."

"He seems an honest man."

"Sure is. That's why those young cock-wavers can't stomach him. Moment Thaddeus dies or moves on, then Pine's Peak goes with him. And that's the damned truth, Apache. Since the trains never came, the place's been like a man on the edge of the drop, keeping hold with his fingertips. Sheriff goes and the town lets go."

"What about you?"

Cuchillo had moved close to the bars, standing easy and relaxed. He saw the leather purse and his golden knife lying side by side on the desk. The few poor possessions of the old Utes were with them—nothing but some small change and a couple of narrow skinning knives. He allowed his headband to dangle in his good left hand, almost as though he'd forgotten it.

Almost.

"Now you sure 'bout some water? I'm about to get me some sleep, and I feel bad about not doin' something for you poor bastards. Never harmed me much."

Tardy and Cuchillo were face to face. The deputy was leaning heavily on his crutch. The tall Apache smiled gently at him. "I think you are not a bad man, Deputy."

The white man came close to blushing. "Well . . . I don't rightly. . . . Thank you kindly for that." He paused. "I sure wish there was somethin' that I could do to help you . . . but you . . . Hell, you. . . ."

"There is something."

"Sure. What? I could maybe rouse out some grits to go with that pork." He laughed, the laughter

38

turning into a coughing fit that doubled him over. His face turned red, his eyes watered, his fingers were clawing at the palms of his hands as he fought for breath.

Cuchillo watched him in silence, turning once to look at the other Indians in the cell. They both stayed still, staring back at him without the least flicker of expression on their faces.

"Hellfire and bastard death!" spat Tardy, finally regaining control. "Get that stinkin' chokin', and I run clean out of breath. Where was we?"

"I asked for something," said the Apache, looking calmly at the crippled old man, who was so eager to please and help. But he was not eager enough to let him out of the jail and save his life.

"What?"

"That." Cuchillo pointed past him to the desk, and Tardy turned to look and see what it was that the Indian wanted.

Less than a half minute after that Deputy Dave Tardy of Pine's Peak was dead.

CHAPTER FIVE

Cuchillo had once met a man from the land of
India, in a border cantina, three-parts drunk and
nearly four-parts dead from a consumption that
spotted the front of his shirt with blood each time he
coughed. They'd started talking, and the conversation had drifted inexorably toward the subject of
death. The little Indian had fled from his homeland,
pursued by the British, to the sea. He was wanted
for a series of religious killings.

He had worshiped a brutal goddess whose name,
as Cuchillo recalled it, was Kali, and he had killed
for her. But the way he had done it fascinated the
Apache. Despite his illness, the dark-skinned assas-
sin had shown him the skill—the art of the "toog"
or "thug," of strangling in the dark from behind by
using only a long scarf and a silver coin to weight
one corner. The Indian had tied a dollar in the long
scarf he wore around his neck. He was standing behind Cuchillo, who had been braced and ready to
parry the attack. But the Apache had been too slow.
There had been the faintest hissing in the air, and

then it was as though a powerful snake had locked itself around his windpipe. The thug had snatched the loose end as it whipped around, locking Cuchillo's wrists and pulling. It wasn't hard enough to kill, though he was very drunk, but it pulled hard enough to earn the tall warrior's grudging admiration.

One of the things that Cuchillo Oro was very good at was remembering what mattered. He never bothered to clutter up his mind with useless facts, but when something came along that might one day be of some use to him, then it was locked firmly away.

While he'd been lying on the bunk, playing with the few coins left to him, the Apache had contrived to knot them into one corner of his long cotton headband, which he was holding loosely in his hand as he talked to the deputy. The weight hung low, and Cuchillo took care that he didn't allow it to clink against the bars. Then, as Dave Tardy turned away from him and looked back into the office, Cuchillo had made his move. He was as fast and lethal as a prairie rattler so that the white man died not truly knowing what had happened to him.

Tardy had looked across, seeing only the great golden hilt of the cinqueda gleaming in the light from the oil lamp. It was a beautiful object. The rough gold was studded with semi-precious stones, and he wondered if the Apache seriously expected him to hand it over.

Then he was choking. The familiar tightness was gripping his throat, squeezing the breath from his lungs, making him blink in shock at the suddenness and speed of the attack. Doc Whiteside had warned him that he might get a shortness of breath if he carried on smoking at the rate he did, but he hadn't expected it to be so total.

He opened his mouth to try and speak, but the pressure was too great, making his eyes water. He seemed stuck to the bars, and he struggled to move. As his jaw gaped, he was barely aware of something around his neck, locking him upright like a steel band. It had to be the arm of that big Apache who'd wanted . . . what? Something he'd . . . He was holding him upright, supporting him.

Tardy's eyes closed, and his tongue protruded black and swollen from his crimson lips. His eyes opened again and blinked furiously, feeling as if they threatened to burst out of their sockets. It was awful, more painful than any attack he'd ever had. His chest was heaving for breath and not finding any through the constricted windpipe.

Cuchillo held him tight, hands locked behind the man's neck. Behind him he was aware that both Utes had risen to their feet at the sight of the attack, but they presented no threat, and he ignored them.

Tardy's foot stamped on the floor like a petulant child, and his hands groped at Cuchillo's forearm, which was clamped across his throat. Tardy touched it and felt relieved that someone was saving him from toppling to the boards. The keys jangled furiously as he jerked and tugged, and his crutches fell away from him, rattling against the back of the desk.

Blackness was closing in on Dave Tardy, and his last conscious thought was of gratitude to the big

Apache for supporting him through the final crippling attack of breathlessness.

His lips moved, and his brain tried to form the words "Thank you," but the lines were down throughout his body, and he died without uttering them. His arms relaxed, and his leg dangled limp. Cuchillo lifted him clear of the floor and held him easily with the scarf knotted tight. He gave a final mighty squeeze that snapped the white man's neck. As the deputy died, he fouled himself. The Apache dropped him, taking care that the dead man fell conveniently close to the cell door so that he could reach through the bars, unhook the keys from the corpse's belt and drag them inside.

"We go," said Wounded Bear, joining him by the door.

"It was good killing," muttered Crooked Eye, whose hands were twitching with his eagerness to get through the door and away into the darkness beyond the jail.

All three of the Indians knew with a total certainty that if they were caught anywhere at all after the killing, they would be dead men.

"Come," said Cuchillo, still panting from the effort of strangling the cripple. He stepped out across the sprawled body and dropped the keys alongside it. The two old men followed him out of the cell, one stumbling as he tripped over the discarded crutches.

"Where do we go?" asked one of the Utes.

"You go where you wish," Cuchillo replied, using English.

"We go with you."

"No."

"We are brothers."

"We are not brothers, old man. I run and kill alone."

Wounded Bear shook his head sorrowfully, picking up his knife and sliding it back into the sheath at his belt. "Young men not respect elders."

Cuchillo struggled for the words in the Ute language, for he understood it far better than he spoke it. But he gave up the fight and reverted yet again to his stilted English.

"You are too old to run with me. Old men should lie by fires and talk of old hunts and drink."

Crooked Eye walked to the window that overlooked the street, pulling the corner of the drapes back with an exaggerated caution. Cuchillo noticed for the first time that he limped badly; he favored one foot as if he had an old ankle injury. The two Utes, dressed in bygone styles, looked like a couple of decrepit scarecrows.

"White not come. No noise. We have time run far and fast." Crooked Eye's English was as feeble as he was, creaking like a rusty gate, long unused.

"I will help you to hide. Then, when the leaders of the hunt are not so hot, we may all leave."

"We head off for reservation," said Wounded Bear, turning quickly so that his necklace of soldiers' knuckle bones rattled.

"You are a foolish old man whose belly is larger than his cunning," sneered Cuchillo.

The warrior dropped his hand to the skinning knife. He drew it with a fluent ease, his mind controlling the action so well that the aging body coped with it.

"I kill you Apache," he snarled, back in his own tongue. "Your hair will decorate my lodge, and my squaws will spit in your open mouth."

"The white-eyes will follow your trail as easily as following a wounded buffalo through a swamp. They will know where your feet carry you."

Crooked Eye grinned at his old friend. "You have no squaws, and your lodge poles are falling down."

Cuchillo ignored the cackling laughter of the limping Ute and looked around the desk for some paper and a pen. "I will tell them that the killing was mine," he said, finding what he wanted. He laboriously licked the steel penpoint. The flat metallic taste took Cuchillo instantly back to the little mission school where John Hedges had drummed the rudiments of writing into his head.

"Guard the door," he said, not that he looked for any interruption so late. Crooked Eye obeyed his instructions, and Wounded Bear went behind him, toward the cells, clearly still sulking. His skinning knife was unsheathed in his right hand.

Writing had always been a grim battle for the young Apache. He fought for mastery over the scrawling black shapes that tried to run beyond his control and even vanish off the edges of the paper. He pressed his tongue between his even teeth and struggled on.

"Sheriff Mann," he began. "Depputie kild by me, Cuchillo Oro, and not by old men in prisson." He hoped that it might be enough to keep the hounds

46

off their trail and save the Utes from further harrying. But from what he had seen of the so-called justice of the white men, he doubted it. However it was all that he could do for them.

As he finished the note and looked at it, ready to lay it in the center of the desk, Cuchillo heard a sickeningly familiar sound behind him. It was a ripping noise that could hardly be mistaken from anything else. He remembered, as a young buck, seeing a friend with a chest infection being treated by the wife of a passing missionary. She had applied a sticky plaster of mustard and pepper and garlic and oil firmly to his friend's chest, telling him to leave it for three days. She returned at the appointed day and made him lie down. She had set her feet astride him to the amusement of the rest of the tribe, who called out ribald comments that passed uncomprehended by the woman. She had taken the plaster in both hands and tugged at it. The ripping noise was so like another sound, that every warrior there had fallen instantly silent.

His friend had died two days later.

Cuchillo looked slowly around, knowing what he was going to see. Crooked Eye giggled his merriment from by the window as Wounded Bear straightened painfully up and slid his bloodied knife back into its sheath. He shook the scalp. Grizzled hair was matted with gouts of crimson blood that dripped onto the planks. Wounded Bear grinned at Cuchillo as he tucked the hair into his belt.

"White man pay good for scalp. Not know who belong to."

That had been the noise. Cuchillo had taken hair

a few times in his life, but generally for revenge—
never just for money or for honor. Honor was a
word that meant little these days to the lone
Apache, who operated as he did totally outside any
tribal society. The old man had done it well, without
fumbling.

He'd cut deeply, drawing the knife across the top
of the temples, following the line where the hair
would have been on a man younger than poor dead
Tardy. He'd pulled it through the skin of the wrinkled forehead, slicing from left to right, then across
above the ears and clean around the rear of the
skull. Blood was flowing freely.

After that came the noise.

Wounded Bear had inserted his rheumatic-bent
fingers into the cut at the front of the head, pressing
in his nails to ensure that he had a good grip. He
turned the corpse on its face and knelt slowly by the
shoulders, using all of his strength to rip the scalp
off the top of the skull in one neat piece.

It was a sound that you didn't forget once you'd
heard it.

Having taken his own knife back, as well as the
leather wallet with a few dollars in it, there was no
reason for staying. Cuchillo walked quietly to the
bolted door at the rear of the building. He eased it
open and peered out into the darkness. Far off in
the distance he could hear the lonesome wailing of a
coyote, but the town itself was silent as a grave.

"You take guns," said Wounded Bear.

"No. That makes more trouble."

"Guns make us safe. We kill many, many white-eyes," grinned Crooked Eye, brandishing a battered Winchester. He levered a round into the breech. The Apache wondered whether the old man was about to start shooting off a few bullets as a token celebration. If he had even fired a single shot, Cuchillo would have taken out his throat with the great knife before leaving for the high peaks of the Colorado Territory.

The other old man had also found himself a rifle and was waving it triumphantly at the Apache, his face cracked with pleasure at the exciting adventure that they were all having.

"It is like the old times, brothers," croaked Wounded Bear. "We shall drink of the blood of enemies. And it will be as the hunting of the mighty white buffalo. The spirits will watch us."

"Ayiee, but it is surely a good day to die on," said Crooked Eye, his voice rising toward a shout.

Cuchillo turned to him and raised a finger to his lips. "There is a bad moon rising that will make it easy to track us," he said. Some of his half-remembered grasp of the Ute tongue was returning to him. "We must leave now. Bring the guns."

They slipped away into the night, disappearing into the brush that grew up close to the backs of the buildings on the main street.

At a little after 6 A.M. sheriff Thaddeus Mann walked slowly along that street toward the jail. He paused to exchange a few words with a couple of women, commenting on what a fine morning it looked like. He stopped once more by the livery stables to check that nobody had entered or left the

49

town since he'd gone out to his home the previous evening. Thaddeus Mann was a thorough peace officer, and he liked to know that kind of thing.

But there was no word of any strangers around Pine's Peak. That was generally the way nowadays. If only the tracks had reached . . . ventured the owner of the stable, Hiram MacArthur, as he did most mornings. It was a part of the day the lawman would have missed if he hadn't said it.

The sun was dazzling, throwing sharp shadows from the angled corners of the roofs, drying the overnight dew from the street so that his boot heels crunched as he walked. The sheriff's mind was partly on his dream of the previous night. He wondered how long the gibbering phantoms of the War would plague him. He wondered if there was any way at all that he might find some kind of peace of mind.

Part of him was also considering what he would do with the big Apache. He should hold him for 30 days, but he didn't like the idea. And he knew well enough that the young lads who were his deputies would have him dead within a week.

"What the hell," he muttered. There'd been times when he'd have worried a lot about that, but now he was getting older, and it was harder to care. It was one Indian less to worry about.

He stopped a few paces short of the office and eased the Colt on his hip, sucking on a hollow tooth as he looked around him. He had a small, private wager with himself that Dave Tardy would be fast asleep and not hear him call.

"Hello, the jail! Hello, the jail!" His voice echoed

around the buildings. Near half of them were showing signs of wear and tear, with the end three already leaning drunkenly to one side, long empty and abandoned.

"Hello in there! Come on, Dave, it's me." His crippled deputy was becoming less and less reliable. It wasn't that he lacked the balls for the job, but he was just getting too damned old.

Sheriff Mann finally stepped up onto the porch. He suddenly noticed that the drapes were still pulled across the barred windows at the front of the jail. Something pricked at the base of his spine, and he reached down, flicking the thong that held the Colt safely in its Mexican rig at his hip. He cautiously pushed the door open and walked inside.

He was in the building for less than one minute, and when he came out, his eyes were as cold as melting water. He looked up and down the street, and his lips moved, mouthing a single word.

"Bastard!"

CHAPTER SIX

John Hedges had once tried to convince Cuchillo that if you wanted to hide something, then the best place was out in the open where people least expect it. The young Apache had laughed at him.

"Cuchillo says that even a white man could find a black bear in a schoolroom but not in the deepest darkness of the forest." Hedges had shaken his head and given it up as a bad job, knowing that there were certain areas of life in which the teenager could teach him things far more vital than multiplication tables or spelling rules.

But now where could he hide a couple of crazy old men in a slowly dying town? That was far more of a problem for the Apache. There was a great temptation to ditch the Utes and make a run for it, but they would know the local ground better than he did. And besides, though he had lived beyond the tribal customs for a long time, Cuchillo still felt an instinctive need to protect the aged warriors from harm as best he could.

But that instinct was speedily wearing thin. Both

Crooked Eye and Wounded Bear seemed to look upon what was happening as if it were just a merry boys' prank, and they chattered together as they made their way to the north of the settlement, breaking through the dry brush at the sides of the gulches like wounded buffalo. Cuchillo did everything he could to keep them quiet, finally quieting them by the threat of leaving. It was good for the aged warriors to have such a powerful young buck along with him, and they finally lapsed into a slightly sullen silence. However both found it hard to move as quietly or carefully as the Apache wanted.

"Are the Ute women heavy with child that they leave a trail a blind white soldier could follow?" Cuchillo hissed angrily.

They walked through a narrow stream, staying in the middle of it, only leaving the bubbling water when a shelf of bare rock presented itself to their right. Cuchillo helped them up onto it with much puffing and panting and then waited until they had gathered their breath again.

"Where is a place the whites will not think to search?" he asked.

"Caves," suggested Crooked Eye, panting hard, one hand on his chest.

"No."

"Old iron-road caves?" tried Wounded Bear.

"No," rejected Cuchillo, shaking his head. It would be dawn before long, and the town would start to boil like a broken ants' nest.

"There is a . . . house of their gods," Crooked Eye said, pointing up the hill behind them.

"A church?"

"Yes, that is their word."

It was difficult to see as the moon kept vanishing behind scudding clouds, but Cuchillo was just able to make out a building where the Ute pointed. It seemed more solid than most frontier churches that he had seen.

"It is wood?"

Wounded Bear shook his head, coughing and spitting in the dirt. "It is stone. When iron road come, then white men have pride and build well."

It sounded like a possibility. It crossed Cuchillo's mind that the town's people, with their unhealthy Christian ritual of burial of the dead, might be up to see the last of Dave Tardy. But he remembered that it was often a day or so before the interment. That should be long enough.

"There is room at top where we go to drink in summer. Not hot and quiet there. No men come," said Crooked Eye.

"And see town and trail well," added Wounded Bear, hefting the rifle meaningfully.

"Come," said the Apache. He led the way up the steep side of the hill toward the church. After climbing over a low stone wall, he found himself in among rows of graves that were rock-covered to keep out the dogs and other animals. Some had markers of stone; a few were marked with rotted wood. The cemetery was sadly overgrown with weeds, which were springing up everywhere, obscuring the neat paths and trim organization.

The old men were struggling far behind him, and Cuchillo didn't wait for them. He picked his way, cat-footed, among the stones, pausing when he was in the shadow of the building. He flattened himself against the gray wall. It was a substantial church, right enough. He stared up at it, seeing the tower with slots for windows, and he guessed that it would indeed make a splendid observation post, but without much chance of escape if you got yourself trapped up there.

The door was wood, its metal handle missing. Cuchillo pushed at it, and it swung open, making only the slightest creaking sound. Inside the air smelled cool and damp with a hint of some other odor. He wrinkled his nose, trying to identify it.

"Whisky," he said. The Utes had mentioned that they used the church for their drinking sessions—a room at the top they had said.

The moon barely reached inside through the high, narrow windows, and he held his hands out in front of him and felt a wooden bench. And another. There was the faintest of drafts coming from his left, and he walked in that direction. He heard sniggering and crashing as the two old men made their way to the entrance.

"Quiet," he called.

"Who speaks?" asked Crooked Eye.

Wounded Bear replied with an imitation of an owl—a good one, the Apache admitted to himself.

"That was how we caught that old man and his daughter. Back in the year that the water came above the line of tallest trees and Man Whose Pony Danced was killed by the soldiers."

Cuchillo fumbled around the inside of the church, nearly knocking over a stack of books thick

56

with dust, listening with part of his mind to the reminiscences of the elderly warriors. He was concentrating most of his mind on following the elusive draft.

"The old man whose hair was long and burned in the wind?"

"Yes. Whose daughter wept as we honored her."

There was another door, which was nearly closed. As Cuchillo approached it, he could hear the sound of the wind sighing through the crack. It had to be the way up to the church tower.

"Her blood was so bright in the sun. I was first to take her," said Crooked Eye.

"No. I was."

"Me."

"It was me," insisted Wounded Bear, his voice cracked with senile anger.

"I was the first between us," shouted Crooked Eye.

Both of the old men had totally forgotten where they were and what danger they were all in, with a scalped deputy lying dead in the town below them. Cuchillo knocked on the tower door with the haft of his golden knife. The sudden echo silenced them.

"Hold your tongues, or we are all to die," he said, the chill rage in his voice penetrating the quarrel of the Utes.

"She killed herself the next day. Drowned in the creek," said Wounded Bear, very quietly. The contentment in his voice indicated that he had managed to have the final word in the discussion.

The door opened stiffly, as though there was a small animal lying against it, and the smell of the cold night air came more clearly, but with that over-lying stink of whisky. Cuchillo began to climb. He heard Wounded Bear lumbering behind him, still muttering to himself. Crooked Eye's old ankle injury was making him slower and clumsy.

"Beware of the broken glass," said the leading Ute.

"What?"

"There are many smashed bottles there. But much clear space."

"We always broke them in one place," added Crooked Eye, panting with the effort of the climb.

Cuchillo felt his way to the top, pausing when his hand encountered no further stairs. He stepped carefully out and saw a faint light from the slits in the room. He walked across and peered out in the direction of Pine's Peak. Cuchillo was wondering if the corpse had yet been found, but the township was silent and dark. The moment Tardy was discovered, then all hell would break loose, and the country around them would likely be scoured by an armed posse.

"We can kill from here without being seen with these guns," suggested Wounded Bear, knocking into Cuchillo in the darkness. He sighed as he lowered himself to his haunches and squatted against a wall.

"They will see the smoke of the bullets," snapped the Apache, contemptuously.

"Then we will sit and wait," added Crooked Eye. From the corner where he was standing, Cuchillo heard the pattering of water as the old man relieved himself.

"If we had some drink . . . ," sighed Wounded Bear, "the time would go quicker. How long we wait?"

"A day, old man. Perhaps two. We can slip out for food and drink after a day. It is good there is no whisky. It makes a man careless. I will sleep now. One must watch."

"Me," they both said together.

Sensing another of their interminable arguments, Cuchillo stopped them. "Perhaps you can watch together. It is not long to first light."

And so they waited.

Both the Utes dropped off to sleep within a half hour of the Apache. None of them were awake at the moment when Sheriff Thaddeus Mann went into his jail down the hill from the church, and then reappeared a few moments later.

What woke them was the first shot.

Cuchillo jerked immediately from sleep, rising from a tortured dream about Captain Cyrus Pinner and his own long-dead wife and child. The nightmares still plagued him even though he had ended his feud with the Cavalry officer in the most final way possible.

It had been a single shot. Then came another, the flat sound bouncing back from the hills on the farther side of Pine's Peak. Wounded Bear was sliding back from sleep, flat on his back in the dirt. The darkness of the tower was split by sharp-edged spears of light that thrust in from the slots in the walls.

Crooked Eye slept on, half on his side. His mouth sagged open, showing a few rotting teeth, which supported a whole lot of gaps. Breath came moaning from his throat, and he twitched at the second shot, still not waking.

Cuchillo moved to the nearest window, nearly falling over an old mattress and a pile of stained blankets in the corner. It was a bigger room than he'd thought, with a pair of large pillars that split it in two. There was a great mound of broken glass in the farther corner, the jagged shards of whisky bottles glinting viciously as the sun brushed them. It was an impressive sight. The two Utes must have been coming here for years to have accumulated so much glass. There was also evidence around that white men came here for privacy, the crusted stains on the blankets telling their story, with the discarded butts and paper showing the race.

But the Apache was far more interested in what was going on below him. By standing flat against the wall and easing his face to the slit, he could see that Tardy had been found. Over the rocks and the fringe of trees, Cuchillo could see clear to the main street. There was the tall, gray-haired figure of Mann holding his hat in one hand, a pistol in the other. Even as he looked down, the lawman raised the gun and fired off a third shot, the coil of smoke rising lazily in the still morning air.

There were three or four men with him, and even in the minute or so that the Apache stared unblinkingly down, another half dozen appeared. He could recognize the beanpole shape of Albie Chesterman loping along, his shadow incredibly long and thin ahead of him. It was obvious that Thaddeus Mann was in the process of rousing a posse.

"They find body?" grunted Wounded Bear, who lumbered across and kicked his old friend in the ribs, making him cry out. "Wake, Crooked Eye. The whites come soon."

"No?"

"No," said Cuchillo, moving away from the window, knowing that there would be many moments that the hunters' eyes would scan the hills and woods for a glimpse of them. Any movement could give them away. "Keep back and out of sight. Get your guns ready but *do not* set the hammers. Leave them against the wall. I do not wish there to be any mistakes."

And so they waited.

They used dogs to try to find them, but the scent disappeared when the Indians had entered the water, and, although the three could see the men casting around for it, there was no further trace on the bare rocks.

It was just like Cuchillo Oro had guessed it would be. There seemed to be men riding and running everywhere. The Utes would crawl over, shuffling through the dust, and peer out of one of the windows. They muffled their laughter by sticking their fists in their mouths. Tears rolled down their wrinkled, leathery cheeks at the spectacle of the white men so wildly aroused.

The Apache was interested to see that most of the search seemed to be concentrated over by the old railroad where Wounded Bear and Crooked Eye

61

had suggested they might hole up. Mann appeared two or three times, once riding a bay mare among the trees at the bottom of the path that led up to the church. But not once did his face turn toward the stone building, and nobody came that way. As far as Cuchillo could make out, the bulk of the effort was being spent on covering all the trails out of Pine's Peak. As there were only two—one in and one out—that wasn't too difficult.

They saw Dave Tardy's body being carried out of the jail, wrapped in a gray blanket, watched by a curious crowd of women and small children. Albie Chesterman was conspicuous as he whipped up a mob of about 15 young men, lathering his horse as he spurred it up and down the street, his spurs speckling the animal's flanks with blood. Larry Feathers stayed mainly on foot. His shirt was peeled open to the waist so that the ladies and young girls could admire his muscular physique. Sheldon Green was there as well, driving a buckboard and pausing every now and again to brandish a length of rope above his head—a length of rope that ended in a hastily made hangman's noose.

Cuchillo hadn't seen any sign of Pete Green, the more talkative of the twins.

The hunters carried on all through the morning. Some of them broke off in shifts, Cuchillo noticed, for a snatched meal around noon. As the afternoon wore on, it was clear that their enthusiasm was waning. The three Indians saw a handful of them sitting stretched out in the shade of the trees near the stream, smoking and joking. The feeling must be flowing among the town's people that the Utes and the Apache had gotten clean away, and they were wasting their time.

As the sun shifted, so its rays came in through different slots and glittered across the small mountain of broken bottles in the corner of the tower. Cuchillo lay down and closed his eyes. He still felt tired and in need of some sleep. The days leading up to his arrival in Pine's Peak hadn't been that easy, and his body craved some ease.

"Keep watch, and this time don't sleep," he told the two old men, looking at them sternly. "Not like last time. I would trust you as brother warriors."

The flattery worked, and Wounded Bear and Crooked Eye took turns looking out over the town. Then they started to play a Ute game involving tossing up small stones and catching them again on the back of the hand. They became involved in it, kidding each other for being clumsy. Their concentration on being guards soon slipped away from them.

But they still played in near silence; they took care not to disturb the big Apache as he lay asleep. They had moved behind one of the pillars in the tower room so they wouldn't bother him—their rifles clear away on the farther side of the attic.

The afternoon dragged on, and each time one of them peered out across the settlement, there seemed to be less and less enthusiasm for the hunt. Only Sheriff Mann and the skinny Albie Chesterman still kept their eagerness, urging on the rest of the men. But there was an air of resignation that their prey had escaped them. So the Utes kept playing, out of sight of the top of the stairs, and Cuchillo Oro kept on sleeping.

None of them heard the careful feet in the long grass among the graves. Nor the slight creak as the main door of the church was pushed slowly open. Nor the rustling of a dress against the pews, or the boots on the floor. They didn't hear the other door opening, the feet cautiously clambering up the stairs to the top of the tower.

Just the triple click of a Colt being cocked and a man's surprised voice.

"Holy shit, Marianna! Look what we got!" said Pete Green, triumphantly.

CHAPTER SEVEN

When the Civil War had finally ground itself to a bloody halt, Pine's Peak was like hundreds of other small communities all across the reunited states of America. Several of its youngest and best were gone, and all that remained were widows and orphans, young girls and older men. One reason that Albie, Hoss and the Green twins had managed to get such a grip on the township was that there were virtually no other lads of their age left alive and unmaimed in the area—which meant that it wasn't difficult for Pete Green, despite the nest of pimples that circled his mouth, to be fairly successful with the girls. And if you were a honed blade like Larry Feathers, then the young ladies just fell smiling into your hands like a cartload of ripened peaches.

The tower of the old church was only used for an occasional funeral or even less frequent wedding. It was an ideal place for a lover's tryst—not that the four deputies ever called their assignations by such a romantic name. Generally, they were referred to as "tearing off a slice of white meat" or "ramming the cunts with both barrels." None of them was very romantically inclined. Since the death of Pine's Peak's only minister, the Reverend John McLaglen, who had died of frostbite that became gangrene four winters back, the church was almost totally deserted. The boys knew that the Utes used it for summer drinking, but that was in the day, and the Indians were long out of it by nightfall, considering it probably haunted.

Pete Green had taken very little part in the hunt for the Apache and the other two old men. He had seen enough of Cuchillo Oro and had heard enough of the legend of the cunning and cruelty of Pinner's Indian to be wary of risking his life by going after him.

And all for Dave Tardy. He'd said as much to Sheriff Mann; he'd said more, in fact. He'd whined as they started a third sweep along the railway tracks, "What's the point of this just for one fuckin' old cripple?"

As he walked through the graveyard with Marianna Grange, daughter of the retired schoolteacher, Pete Green had experimentally touched his tongue to the swelling inside his lip where Thaddeus Mann had slapped him, open-palmed, knocking him on his back in the dirt and the silence. Two of his front teeth still felt loose.

But that was forgotten as he stood triumphantly in the tower. His pistol was in his hand, with its barrel pointed safely at the figure of the big Apache. His girl was at his side, admiring his courage. It was a great moment—perhaps the greatest of his young and rather brutish life.

And it was to be one of his last.

"Get up, and real slow, bastard," he snarled.

Cuchillo sat up, back against the cool stone. He wondered for a moment where the two Utes were. Then he saw a flash of movement behind the pillar and guessed that they'd been caught. He thought they'd been asleep, and even though they hadn't, the end result was much the same.

The Apache recognized the boy immediately. He looked curiously at the girl and realized when he saw her that it was sheer luck they'd been found. Green and Marianna had paused for a cuddle in the church, and her right breast still protruded from the front of her bodice, quite forgotten in the excitement.

"I don't rightly know, Mister Gold Knife, whether to put a bullet through your murderin' guts here and now, or hold you for a real legal lynchin'."

"Shoot him now, Pete," urged the girl, wide-eyed with the thrill.

"Guess I should after what he done to poor old Dave Tardy." The "fuckin' old cripple" had somehow slipped from his mind. "Maybe a couple through his belly, huh?"

Cuchillo didn't speak. He shuffled a little so that he could get a good grip with his feet on the floor, ready to power himself across the space. There were about eight feet between the boy and the Apache. Could he beat a bullet across that far?

"Shoot him in the balls, Pete," whispered the girl. "I'd surely like to see that."

The deputy grinned. "I'd oblige you, Marianna. I could make him take off his breeches first."

She clapped her hands at the idea. "Oh, that would be just dandy, Pete. I'd let you do anythin' you wanted to me if'n you'd do that. You wouldn't let me do the shootin', would you?"

Green hesitated, his eyes never leaving his prisoner. It was a tempting offer, but he had enough sense left to realize that it would be difficult to give her the gun without also giving the Indian a chance at him—unless he put a couple of bullets through his knees first. That'd slow him some.

Cuchillo still held back his move. A man who's talking isn't shooting. Suddenly, around the pillar behind the young couple, he saw the face of Wounded Bear, then his shoulders and an arm. He was holding a chunk of broken wood as large as a man's thigh, hefting it with difficulty. His cheeks were red with the effort. But he was grinning over Pete Green's shoulder at the Apache, nodding his encouragement to show that Cuchillo was not alone and rescue was right at hand.

Cuchillo couldn't signal to the old Ute to stay out of it. If he swung and missed, as was more than likely, then the white man would certainly gun down Cuchillo and probably Wounded Bear and Crooked Eye in the bargain.

"Guess I'll cripple him, Marianna, then you can have a go at him. Take off your pants, Indian! Right now, or else I'll . . ."

Wounded Bear had taken a silent step nearer, and Cuchillo saw the other old man behind him, smiling and nodding his enthusiasm for their rescue.

Time was slipping away faster than dry earth in a flash flood.

Slowly, taking care not to frighten the boy into pulling the trigger, Cuchillo stood up. His hands fumbled at his belt as if he was obeying the order. Pete Green sniggered nervously, overcome with his own success, scarcely able to believe what a hero he'd become. See what that uppity Sheriff Mann said now!

"Your woman has beautiful breasts," said Cuchillo Oro loudly and clearly, pointing with his right hand at the girl's exposed bosom.

It would have taken a better man than Pete Ephraim Green not to have looked and gaped at what he saw and as he did, the barrel of his Colt wandered off its target. Both the Utes stopped in their tracks, frozen by the words of the Apache.

Ever since he'd been waked, Cuchillo's brain had been racing furiously, calculating odds and working out distances. The sound that would carry farthest would be the explosion of the gun; so that was the first priority. Second came the woman's scream. Anything after that was in the lap of the spirits.

The moment he saw Green's head begin to turn to look at Marianna, the Apache was moving. His left hand went to the familiar hilt of the golden knife, drawing it in a whisper of sound in a frozen fraction of a second. He drove forward across the gap, and the point of the blade raked toward the boy's wrist.

Pete Green saw it coming out of the corner of his eye, but his reactions weren't fast enough. Marianna Grange saw her bare breast, the nipple peaking with

69

tension, her mouth opening to giggle at the wickedness of it all, when she too saw the flicker of movement. She started to step back toward the stairs, the beginnings of a scream starting deep in her throat.

Cuchillo was a devastatingly effective fighting and killing machine. He knew precisely what he was going to do even before he started to move, and everything went more or less like he'd planned.

Even better in some ways.

The tip of the golden knife opened up the deputy's wrist, slicing through the flesh and tendons like a razor through well-cooked chicken breast. Green's gun dropped to the floor in a shower of blood, his fingers extending helplessly. Cuchillo's weight cannoned hard into the boy, which sent him toppling off balance. His heels caught on the edge of the torn mattress so that he staggered back, utterly out of control.

As he moved past her, the warrior kicked out with his left foot at Marianna, hitting her on the knees. She stumbled toward Wounded Bear, who was unable to believe the way the situation had been reversed in a whirlwind moment. The old Ute swung his club at her, striking her a crashing blow on the side of her face.

But if we are going to keep the right order of things, we must now go back to Pete Green.

His hand felt as if it had been plunged into molten metal. He lurched across the tower, flailing his arms but gathering momentum rather than slowing himself down. Finally, he fell flat on his back—in the middle of the pile of needle-tipped broken glass.

For a moment he lay there, unable to believe that

so much pain could exist in the universe. The shards of bottle held him tight, snagging his flesh and clothes, making him terrified to move. Immediately, he could feel the warmth of blood soaking down his back and thighs from a hundred different cuts.

Meanwhile . . . Marianna.

Wounded Bear had broken her jaw with the blow, which almost lifted her off her feet and left her barely conscious. Unable to stand, she slipped silently over the edge of the stairs. They could hear her body as it rolled headfirst down the stone steps, crashing and flailing. There was the clear noise of bones snapping, for she was a slender girl, and then a stillness.

Crooked Eye knew that his old friend would be intolerable to live with unless he did something to match Wounded Bear's sudden success. So he shuffled toward the sprawled figure of Pete Green, licking his wrinkled lips in anticipation of the pleasure to come.

Cuchillo had rolled over on his side and came up on his feet, knife ready for more action. He looked round and saw that it was over.

The girl had disappeared, and from the total silence down the stairs it was unlikely that there'd be any further trouble from her. To remove that scintilla of doubt, the Apache saw Wounded Bear, who was smiling at his success, head for the top of the steps, his skinning knife gripped in his gnarled fingers.

And Pete Green was only a matter of inches from the end of the brief road of life. Helpless, blood soaking the planks all around him, he watched as the crippled Crooked Eye limped at him. He also was holding a knife.

"No. Please don't hurt me. I never. . . . Please . . . don't. They'll find me and . . ."

He tried to move. He groaned as the glass cracked and rustled with a brittle sharpness beneath him, forcing the tiny spears deeper into his back and legs.

"You die, Deputy Green," said Crooked Eye, dragging up his labored words in English. He smiled at the helpless white boy and made him a mocking bow.

"I'll pay. Anything. Take the girl. Do what you like to her."

"You are regular bastard," said Cuchillo, disguestedly. "Not ordinary kind, but special. You live like animal, and you die same way."

The Ute stepped in toward him, but he tripped over the same edge of the mattress and fell on top of Pete Green, his weight making the boy cry out. A strangled moan sent bright blood bubbling from his open mouth. Crooked Eye's body had crushed him so deeply into the broken glass that some of the long, jagged splinters had been forced through his shirt and back and penetrated all the way through to his lungs. Others tore at the side of his neck and throat cutting the jugular vein open, slicing into the carotid artery on the left side of his throat. The blood still pumped furiously from the aorta, but it was failing to reach his brain. Instead, it spilled out in a great fountain of crimson all over Crooked Eye and the glass and half of the tower floor.

The Ute clambered to his feet and pulled his

72

mouth in disgust as he saw the boy was clearly dying.

"I wished to take his life. I would have had the honor of the coup."

"You count coup still," said Cuchillo. "He lived until you attacked him. It was you that slew him, and it is right you claim honor."

That cheered up the old man, and he bent over the corpse with his skinning knife, carefully avoiding the glass as he knelt to take the boy's hair.

Down the stairs Cuchillo heard a ripping sound as the other old man tore the scalp from the head of Marianna Grange.

That was three dead.

The Apache had the grim premonition that the killings had barely begun.

CHAPTER EIGHT

Cuchillo insisted that the girl's corpse be dragged back up the stairs to the safety of the tower. The two Utes did it, struggling and cursing as they pulled the unwieldy body after them. The head banged dully on every step and left a slobbered trail of blood behind it from the scalp and from the slit throat. They threw her casually on top of the dead boy, laughing as the two bodies seemed to tangle together in an obscene parody of a lovers' embrace.

The rest of the afternoon passed less happily.

Within the hour the corpses were beginning to smell, and by the time the sun was dipping below the high peaks away to the west of the town, the tower stank like a summer slaughterhouse. Flies were attracted by the scent of blood and buzzed incessantly about the bodies, dipping themselves delicately into the congealing pools, swarming over the scattered glass.

Cuchillo kept a more careful watch, but he didn't expect any real trouble until later. The time would come during the evening when Pete Green and the girl would be missed, and then the search would begin all over again. Their meeting place was probably well-known by the other three boys, and the first place checked would be the tower of the deserted church. By that time it would be well to put some distance between themselves and the corpses.

As soon as dusk came crawling reluctantly across the land, Cuchillo stood by the slotted window overlooking the settlement, keeping careful watch for any threatening sign of action. But the place was quiet. In twos and threes the posses came in, horses head-down, men slumped in saddles, their rifles safely bucketed. A lamp was lit outside the jail, and Sheriff Thaddeus Mann sat in an old rocking chair. He had a ten-gauge scatter-gun across his lap, and was taking in the news from each returning party. Over the period of a half hour that he watched, Cuchillo saw the other three young deputies reporting in. Nobody seemed to have missed Pete Green yet, but it could only be a matter of time before questions were asked about the boy.

The township gradually disappeared in the evening dimness, and Cuchillo moved from the window. He picked up Green's gun, checked that it was fully loaded and stuck it in his belt. The Utes had been sitting quietly, again playing their game. They creaked to their feet at the signal from the Apache. Wounded Bear had two scalps dangling from his belt, and Crooked Eye the one.

"This is as the old times, Cuchillo Oro," said the fatter of the old men.

"Aye, it is so. To feel the hair of a white dog beneath the knife is good," added Crooked Eye.

"The old times ended in death for many," commented Cuchillo. "Let us take care."

"Where do we go?"

"Circle around the town toward the old railway," said Cuchillo. "They have looked there and will not search again."

"We kill more."

"No, Wounded Bear. Cuchillo says that a lone moose does not challenge the pack of wolves."

"Why not stay here for the night?"

"I would not be trapped here by the whites if they come after those," explained Cuchillo, pointing at the fly-smothered bodies. "I would fight in the open where we can have more chance."

"It will be a fine battle, Cuchillo Oro," grinned Crooked Eye, limping across to the top of the stairs, carrying the rifle in his right hand.

"Many will die," called Wounded Bear. He shook his fist. The action made his necklace of knuckle bones quiver and rattle.

"I will be happy if there are no deaths," said Cuchillo grimly, wondering yet again whether he might not do well to leave the two old men to their phantom pasts and their uncertain futures. But he found something almost endearing in the way they constantly refused to give in.

Despite all the odds, the Utes were survivors, sad relics of their once-proud tribe.

They made their way through the cemetery with Cuchillo leading. He stepped cautiously in case the lawman was cunning enough to leave sentries behind, hidden. But he guessed that Mann would simply think they had headed back for the reservation and therefore wasn't taking too many precautions. Once they found the bodies of the girl and Pete Green, then things would change. Thaddeus Mann didn't seem the sort of person to sit back after having had two of his deputies killed within 24 hours.

"Move quietly. I think men come this way. Yes, down and stay silent."

The two old warriors obeyed him, lowering themselves slowly and painfully into the thick brush close to the side of the stream. They were not far from the main street of town.

It was the sheriff himself, leading about a dozen men, walking fast toward the trail up to the church. The three young men were with him. Sheldon Green was in the lead and was chattering excitedly to Mann.

Most of the houses and stores in the settlement were lit up, and Cuchillo hoped that neither of the old Utes would give into the temptation to risk a shot or two at the silhouetted men. But the posse walked on by, and the Apache signaled that it was safe to go on.

"Cuchillo."

"What?"

Wounded Bear came waddling up to him, puffing with all the exertion. Crooked Eye was trailing at the rear. He was barely visible as a hobbling shadow against the deeper blackness of the night.

"There is store at the end there where they keep

whisky. It has loose board at rear, and we wish to go and steal bottle each. There is also food."

The thought of having the Utes with him was bad enough, but the prospect of them trailing along after him drunk out of their brains, was terrifying.

"Get food only. Not drink at all. It is too dangerous for us. Bring meat and bread if you can. I will wait one-hundred paces along iron road."

"Whisky?" asked Crooked Eye, who had arrived too late to hear what Cuchillo had been saying. Wounded Bear nudged him in the ribs and whispered something quickly in their own tongue. The young Apache wasn't able to catch what he said, and it roused his suspicions.

"Good. We go and meet you soon."

The people in Pine's Peak would be looking to find the three of them in hiding and wouldn't expect to see them creeping about in the streets. That was Cuchillo's hope. Mann and the other leaders of the hunt were safely out of the way up the hill. As far as he could calculate, using the strange time scales of the white men, Cuchillo expected that they would find the bodies within the next five minutes.

Then the chase would really warm up.

There was a deal of shouting from across the valley, beyond the town. Men were running, and the horses were being spurred toward the church. There was a sudden crackle of shooting and screams. Cuchillo guessed that in the tension of the moment someone had either fired at a friend or at a shadow. From the yelling it sounded as though someone had been hurt.

Cuchillo made his way onward. He stumbled over the first of the old line's rotting ties and rusted rails. He picked his way quickly along to the old tunnel, pausing in the shadows as someone whipped a rig past him on the trail. Voices still yelled out from behind him.

He squatted on his haunches, automatically checking the action on the pistol, making sure that the crawling and running hadn't jarred it. All he could do then was wait for Wounded Bear and Crooked Eye to come with the food. Deep down the Apache didn't really trust the two old Utes to keep their word. Not that they'd actually lie to him, but he was worried about them getting their hands on some liquor and then doing something stupid.

But all he could do was wait and hope that nothing went wrong.

Something went wrong.

The first sign he had was a single shot that cracked out from somewhere among the buildings. The echo rumbled backward and forward between the high cliffs on either side of Pine's Peak. There was a yelp of pain and a burst of gunfire that seemed to be amied from a variety of places. The first shot sounded to Cuchillo's expert ears like it had come from one of the battered rifles that the Indians had been carrying with them.

About ten minutes later he heard panting and rustling in the brush around the farther mouth of the tunnel. He heard the noise of someone falling

80

and the splintering of glass, a muttered curse—and then he saw Wounded Bear.

"Quickly, Crooked Eye. You run like day-old baby with sickness."

From a greater distance: "I am doing my fastest, brother. But my belley is on fire, and I do not see in the great blackness."

Cuchillo's heart sank. Both men sounded as if they were drunk. They were slurring their words, and there had been that sound of breaking glass.

"I have lost the bottle," moaned Crooked Eye, confirming the Apache's worst suspicions.

"It is well. The young one would have been angered with us. Now he will not know."

"True, brother," giggled Crooked Eye. He fell over again, and this time he dropped his rifle in the loose scree at the side of the abandoned track.

"But Golden Knife will be pleased we have killed the man of the law."

"We do not know that Mister Mann is dead."

There was a snort from Wounded Bear. "You rob me of the honor, Crooked Eye. I saw him fall."

"I *thought* I saw him fall."

"Then the honor is . . ."

"And I *thought* I saw him rise."

"When?"

"Holding his shoulder, brother," said Crooked Eye. "I think that your shot hit him but did not kill him."

"It was still well done . . . was it not?" A note of considerable doubt was creeping into the old man's quavering voice.

81

"Golden Knife will not be happy, I think. Not if he knows that we have been drinking whisky."

"Let him cut his own neck with that knife," hissed Wounded Bear. "It is store-bought trash, and I spit upon it."

"Do not speak so, Wounded Bear. He will hear and leave us."

"Let him!" snorted the warrior. "I care not for him."

"Brother!"

"I mean what I say. He is Apache and we are Utes. Are we not better men than he?"

Cuchillo couldn't catch the reply as he was already starting to move silently along the tunnel in the opposite direction from the old men. In the darkness it would have been impossible to have seen his face. But it was set in grim lines of anger and determination—the mouth like a steel trap, eyes cold as flint.

"Where are you, Golden Knife?" crowed Wounded Bear.

"Can you hear us?" echoed Crooked Eye. They both started to move closer to the mouth of the deserted tunnel, their voices becoming deep and distorted by the damp stone roof.

"We are back."

"With great news of a victory over the whites," shouted the limping Ute. His voice dragged among the rough pebbles.

But Cuchillo Oro was no longer where he'd agreed to meet them. Their betrayal of their word by drinking and by trying to kill Sheriff Mann was the final straw for the tall Apache. He now felt that

82

all of his responsibility toward the old men was over. He was heading for his own hiding place.

The Apache left the two Utes, who were blundering helplessly and noisily in the darkness of the tunnel.

Cuchillo Oro was working alone again, moving stealthily back—*into* town.

CHAPTER NINE

Though he hadn't agreed with his old teacher's ideas about hiding, Cuchillo had always believed in trying to do the unexpected to trick the enemy. After the killings in the church they would know that he and the Utes hadn't slipped away through the net and gotten clear of the township. So they must be somewhere around. The posse would start searching the outhouses and barns first, and maybe return to the old railway line.

But they wouldn't be looking in the center of town.

It was easy.

There was still a great disturbance over on the far side of the main street, and Cuchillo was able to snake his way through the shadows, pausing as an old man came muttering out of his house to use the privy at the back of the garden. The Apache crawled on, using the light of the moon to watch for a chance to enter a house.

There it was!

A neat, white-framed building with an attic that overlooked a sloping roof. A trellis had been built along the wall beneath the roof; the dusty remnants of some climbing plants were hanging limply from it. The woodwork looked sturdy enough to bear a man's weight, and the Apache sneaked over the fence. He waited and watched.

There was a light on in the kitchen, visible through the double doors, and he could see a woman bustling about in there, cooking supper. A window was half-open in the kitchen, and Cuchillo breathed in deeply. He could almost taste the freshly baked potato pie and the delicious flavor of some cinnamon apples.

The woman seemed old. She was gray-haired, and she wore a respectable print dress and bonnet. Her sleeves were rolled up above the elbows, her cheeks were dappled with flour from her cooking and baking. She looked like a portrait of an ideal aunt. The rest of the house was quiet.

Cuchillo crept in nearer, flattening himself to the earth behind some currant bushes. All of his nerves were strained on the edge for a sound that might threaten danger. The woman was singing to herself. ". . . Bringing in the sheaves, bringing in the sheaves. . . ."

There was the faint noise of someone rapping on the front door, and the woman disappeared to answer it. Close to the open window Cuchillo could hear the conversation.

"Why, Mr. Bennett."

"Mrs. Hart."

"You're certainly on the dot of the time. And I'm so gosh-darned late."

"I'm surely sorry, Ma'am."

"We mustn't be so formal, Mr. Bennett. You know my given name is Valerie."

"And mine's Frank, Valerie, as well you know."

"Land o'Goshen, but I'm standing here jawin', Frank, and your food's a'spoilin'."

"Sure smells good," said the man. The door closed and feet rang through the house. A lamp was turned up in the back room, and by squinting sideways, the Apache could see a comfortable parlor so filled with furniture it looked as though it was ready to explode. There was a dining table laid for two.

"Land's sakes, but look at me," squeaked the woman as she caught a glimpse of her tousled hair in the mirror that was set at the center of the ebonized overmantel.

"Now, don't get yourself all flustered, Valerie. You go get yourself prettied up, and I'll sit down here and rest. Been a hard day."

The man was in his late 50s. His longish hair, which was whitening at the temples, had been combed carefully across the top of his head to conceal his spreading baldness. He wore a dark suit and vest with a gold chain looped across it. Cuchillo put him down for a banker. On his hip he carried a massive double-triggered Tranter 40-caliber pistol, its butt polished walnut with some inlaid silver.

Cuchillo moved slowly around the house toward the trellis, listening to the conversation of the two elderly people. She was in the kitchen, finishing the meal, though she once scampered up the stairs to the back room and spent a couple of minutes on her hair. The conversation was about the happenings of the day and was carried out in shouts, as they were some distance apart.

Covered by the noise of their talking, Cuchillo began to climb toward the attic window.

"Terrible 'bout poor Dave Tardy, weren't it?"

"Sure was, Valerie, and that's the truth. They took his scalp, you know."

"I heard. My dear friend June told me so. That poor, poor man."

"And now young Green and the Granger girl."

"And someone took a shot at Sheriff Mann, Frank."

"That's so. Winged him in the shoulder. He don't hurt too bad, but he's madder than a boiled rattler at all this."

"Three Ute warriors, I'm told."

"They said there were four or five Apaches with them, all painted for war."

"Land's sakes, but I don't want to think about it. Was the Grange girl . . . ? Had those demons . . . ?"

"I believe so, Valerie."

"They sure better catch them mean devils and string them up good and quick."

"They better," echoed Frank Bennett, sanctimoniously. "I spent the whole day walking my ass . . . pardon me, Ma'am . . . walking in the sun, lookin' for them Indians. Me and the boys don't take kindly to what they've done, and when we find them, we'll surely . . . well, we'll just make certain sure they pay what's owed."

The rest of the conversation faded away as Cuchillo reached the sloping roof. He paused only for a moment to scan the town, conscious that he must make a fine target against the white of the house. Then he cat-footed to the window. It was locked.

"Cuchillo says that a sharp knife is better than most keys," he muttered to himself while concentrating on edging the point of the blade in between the top and bottom frames. He was soon able to slide the catch silently across but had to snatch at the upper half of the window as it suddenly started to fall. The sash cords had snapped, and there was nothing to support it. Grimacing with the effort, the big Indian succeeded in lowering it slowly. He then climbed in over the top and hoisted it shut behind him. After resheathing the golden knife, he took his time to steady his breathing and look around at his hiding place.

It was cluttered and smelled of old dust and locked-away clothes. There was a child's rocking horse with half its mane missing, its studded saddle faded and torn. The moon had shrugged off the clouds and was throwing its clear light through the window, making it easy for Cuchillo to pick his way among the trunks and boxes and stacked pictures.

There were windows on both sides, and he walked carefully across to look out over the street. Mrs. Hart's house was nearly opposite the jail, and he peered through the dusty glass, careful that his face wasn't visible to the men patroling the town. The posses were still bustling around, enlivened by the discovery of the two corpses in the church. There was Sheriff Thaddeus Mann, a white bandage around his upper arm, sitting in a chair, giving orders to the others. Albie Chesterman ran by, preceded by his elongated, questing shadow.

There was a pile of old chenille curtains near the window, and Cuchillo sat down on them to rest for the next day. But something sharp stuck in his back, and he moved a small wooden sled out of the way, its pointed runners red with rust. It had flowers painted on it and a name.

The painting was badly chipped; the last three letters were completely invisible. Cuchillo could only read the first four.

"Rose . . ." he said.

It didn't matter, and he pushed the sled to one side and lay down in the quiet attic.

And so sleep came, as it does to all men, to Cuchillo Oro of the Mimbrenos tribe of Apaches.

He was disturbed by Frank Bennett leaving the house, a little after 11 o'clock. He and Mrs. Hart stayed chattering for several minutes on the back porch, and Cuchillo listened in, hoping he might hear something about the plans of the lawman. But all he learned was that Valerie Hart was a wealthy widow, her husband having succumbed to a fever eight years ago. And Frank Bennett had been courting her manfully ever since. He was a retired banker who had come to Pine's Peak on the promise of the railroad and stayed ever since, getting by on an inheritance left to him by his father back in Indiana.

He tried to kiss her, and she refused him. The eavesdropping Apache learned that he had been trying and she had been refusing him for the last eight years, and it had almost become a game that they both played.

But eventually the elderly man left, and Cuchillo heard the widow Hart readying herself for bed, still singing to herself. "We will gather at the river, the beautiful, the beautiful river. . . ."

The light was turned out, and Cuchillo's sensitive nostrils caught the scent of the smoking wick. Outside there was still activity, with men galloping up and down, carrying flaming torches and shouting to each other. Sheriff Mann had vanished, probably to get himself some sleep the Apache decided. A wound, even if it wasn't a grave one, took it out of you.

It was obvious that they had failed to track down Wounded Bear and Crooked Eye, even though they'd had the hounds out again. Cuchillo shook his head as he watched through the attic window, knowing that tracking dogs were rarely of much use in the darkness. The night seemed to confuse their sense of smell and direction.

Despite having abandoned the Utes, Cuchillo was still vaguely pleased that they had managed to keep out of trouble. And it was with that consoling thought that he slipped into sleep again.

As the false dawn lightened the sky, Cuchillo was awakened by whooping and yells . . . and screams. Even before he rose to look down on the main street, the Apache knew that the hunt was over for the two old warriors. They had reached the end of their trail.

CHAPTER TEN

Cuchillo Oro had never understood the casual enjoyment of the whites in gross violence. The ways of the Indians enveloped torture for captured enemies, with the squaws using their inherited cunning to keep the wretched men alive for three or four days. Using needles and probes and hooks, they would cut and slice at the most delicate parts of a man's body until he was a blind, mewing creature, bereft of any sense beyond the capability to suffer still more pain. But that was understood. It was part of their heritage. The greater the pain for a warrior on the lonely road to death, the greater the honor for him. It was understood.

But the whites had no such tradition. For them it was simply enough to hurt in the crudest and most brutal manner imaginable, with no sense to it.

Cuchillo had observed it before, and it angered him. But in Pine's Peak he was to become more angry than he had been for many years. And his anger would only be cooled in much blood.

* * *

93

There was enough light for him to see clearly what was happening down in the street. There was also enough light for anyone looking up at the attic of the widow Hart's house to spot the shadowed face. But there were some strands of delicate lace curtain yellowed by the Colorado suns, and he carefully tugged them across so that he was veiled from any casual eyes.

Not that anyone was likely to look up from the drama that was being played out to the last scenes, with Wounded Bear and Crooked Eye as the principal, if unwilling, actors. Both of them were still alive, as far as the watching Apache could make out, though both had clearly been badly beaten.

Pete Green's twin brother, Sheldon, was on a horse, with Wounded Bear trussed behind the animal. A cord was tied around his wrists and fastened to the pommel of the saddle. Every time the fat old Ute tried to get to his feet, the boy would whoop and kick the horse forward, dragging the Indian along the street, kicking up a furrow in the dust. Though Wounded Bear was covered in dirt, Cuchillo could see that he was speckled with blood where his clothes had been torn off and the skin rubbed raw.

Being dragged like that wouldn't kill him for some time.

Crooked Eye was walking, hobbling on his weak ankle. His hands were tied behind him and he was being prodded along by Albie Chesterman, who was followed by Larry Feathers. The Ute's face was barely recognizable. It was splotched with crimson, one eye closed, blood running freely from his mouth and nose where he had been either beaten with fists or pistol-whipped.

Thaddeus Mann walked out of the sheriff's office as the Apache looked down. He still carried the scattergun, holding it in his arms as if it were a newborn babe. The crowd had grown until it looked as though all of the citizens of Pine's Peak had come running. Cuchillo heard the front door slam of the house where he was hiding, and he craned his neck to see Valerie Hart. A gown was wrapped about her shoulders like a cloak; she was scurrying barefooted to try and get a good view of the scene.

Mann was holding up his hands, trying to get quiet. Both Indians had been pushed and pulled to the hitching post in front of the small jail. Crooked Eye was leaning against it, being sick, while his friend lay at his feet, rolling about in agony, crying out for . . . Cuchillo couldn't hear what he was crying out for. Mercy? There wouldn't be much of that.

"Quiet!" shouted the lawman. He finally achieved something close to silence by firing off one barrel of the gun, the boom making the window of the attic rattle. Smoke billowed around the gathering at the hitching post.

"That's better. Now, these men are my prisoners, and they'll get a trial."

The howling and shrieking was deafening. During it Crooked Eye managed to help the other Ute to his feet so that they stood together, facing the mob.

"You aim to stop us from hangin' them, Sheriff?" asked a voice from the back of the crowd.

"Guess so."

"They killed Dave Tardy!"

"And the girl."

"Raped her first!"

"Scalped my brother!"

"Killed three of our folks, Sheriff Mann. You can't just let 'em go."

Mann shook his head. "I'm not about to do that, am I? All I say is a legal trial."

"Circuit judge won't be here for months," called Chesterman, who was standing just behind the elderly lawman.

"And those bastards'll be eatin' and gettin' fat on the county. I say hang 'em both!" Cuchillo was able to make out the speaker. It was Frank Bennett. He was waving the Tranter pistol in his pudgy pink fist.

"I have to uphold the law. Take that away, and you got nothing."

Over the years Cuchillo Oro had become skilled in reading between the lines of the white man's speech. He could see what was hidden by the sparkling on the surface. And he knew in his heart the lawman wanted to see Crooked Eye and Wounded Bear dead. Despite his claimed respect for the power of legality, Thaddeus Mann was like everyone else. Having seen his old friend butchered and scalped, then the boy and the girl, he just wished for bloody revenge.

Cuchillo watched silently.

From his brief experience with Mann, the Apache had already come to realize that the lean, grizzled veteran was an exceptional person. There was a quiet self-awareness to him that was rare in white men—a confidence that came from knowing to a hair's breadth just how good he was. Cuchillo admired that in any man.

"I can't stand here and let you take them. I hold to the law."

Behind him, Chesterman suddenly made his move. He pressed the barrel of his Colt to the back of Mann's skull and yelped out his triumph to the mob.

"We know what the old man here wants, and that's what he calls justice. We know a better kind of justice, huh?"

The skinny boy thought that he had manipulated the situation and won control of it. Cuchillo shook his head, breathing quietly in the dusty air. He knew that the lawman had set it up. He'd deliberately stood with his back to the excitable young deputy, sure that he would be goaded into doing something like that. This took the responsibility off Mann's shoulders.

It was cleverly done.

The two Utes were oblivious to what was going on. They simply hung on to each other like a couple of felled trees. Only their own support kept them both from toppling to the dirt. They didn't yet realize that they were quite doomed.

With Albie crowing at his heels, Sheriff Mann turned and walked into the jail. Cuchillo guessed that he would now allow himself to be safely locked away so that he wouldn't have to witness the lynchings.

It was cleverly done.

* * *

In the end it didn't take all that long. The collecting of the kindling took a few minutes, and there was an argument over picking the right tree, which led to a brief flurry of fistfighting. By flattening his face against the cool glass, the Apache was able to see the finish. He strained to make out which men were specially responsible for the brutality.

Revenge was something that had motivated Cuchillo Oro for long years against Pinner, but he had tried to avoid involvement in the problems of others. At that moment he had no strong intention of seeking revenge for the two foolish old men—despite the horrific manner of their passing.

The mob hurried them along, pushing and kicking them. Cuchillo saw a young woman with a baby in her arms reach the front of the crowd and spit in the bloodied face of Wounded Bear. She got a roar of approval from the crowd. Crooked Eye was tripped from behind by a stick held in the hand of a girl no older than 12. Encouraged by some of the men, she climbed on the back of the old warrior and rode him on hands and knees, lashing him with the switch.

At the tree, a huge stump of a sycamore that had been blasted by lightning, both Utes were tied standing with their hands behind them. They were bound around the ankles and thighs and chest and arms, with a final loop tugged brutally tight around their necks. Brush was piled about their legs, reaching nearly to their thighs.

Then there was a silence—an ugly, gloating silence broken only by the crying of the little baby.

Everyone stood there, taking pleasure in what they were about to do to the helpless men.

Larry Feathers was holding a smoking torch, waving it backward and forward so that the wind made the flame roar and sing. Locked in the attic, Cuchillo couldn't make out any words from the lynching mob, but he could hear the sullen animal roaring and screeching. Wounded Bear was hanging in his bonds, barely conscious, but Crooked Eye was alert to what was happening. Cuchillo could see that the old man was trying to shout back at the crowd. And he wasn't begging for life or mercy. At the very last he recovered the pride that the years of white domination had eroded in him.

The pyre was lit.

The flames flared brightly with a pale fire in the early-morning light, and the people of Pine's Peak danced and cheered. They laughed at the way the Utes wriggled and fought against their ropes as they felt the heat scorching their cotton breeches.

Widow Hart bent down, fumbling to pick up a pointed stick from the edge of the fire, its tip scorched and glowing. She stepped in close and held it toward the face of Wounded Bear, delicately lifting the hem of her gown to avoid its becoming blackened by the ashes. She took out the Ute's left eye as neatly as if she were spearing fish on a kitchen spit. Cuchillo could hear the burst of cheering that was her reward. And he could imagine the hissing as the eyeball was burned, and the high cry of pain. Valerie Hart skillfully finished the blinding with a thrust of the pointed stick that would have done credit to a duelist.

Frank Bennett came and put his arm around her and kissed her flushed cheek. The woman with the baby had found a larger piece of burning wood, and she and some of the younger girls took turns poking at the genitals of both old men. They clapped their hands as they burned off the Utes' trousers, gouging at the soft flesh beneath.

Cuchillo turned from the sight, realizing that it was as good a time as any to make his escape from Pine's Peak while the whole town was enjoying its holiday. A burst of shooting stopped him. He looked out once more and saw the banker leading the men in riddling the smoking bodies of the Utes with lead. Bennett was firing the double-action Tranter, the bullets making the Indians buck and twist against the ropes. The flames had reached so high that it was difficult to see properly. The stinking smoke had reached the Apache in the room where he hid and was making him wrinkle his nose in disgust.

Wounded Bear and Crooked Eye hung dead. They bore little resemblance to human beings, standing in the fire like two, large, blackened logs.

"May the spirits receive them into their keeping," muttered Cuchillo Oro. And as he stared down at the bleak street, his eyes suddenly caught something at the far end of the township, away from the lynching.

"No," he said. "No."

CHAPTER ELEVEN

Though he wanted to move from the curtained window, something held Cuchillo Oro there as if he had been nailed into place, unable to remove his eyes from the dreadful scene.

What Pine's Peak had done to Wounded Bear and Crooked Eye was appalling enough, but at least the Apache could see that they thought they had some kind of justification for it. Three people had been killed and scalped. That was a good enough excuse for the burnings.

But it didn't excuse what they did next. Which was why Cuchillo decided that a lesson must be taught to the good citizens of the settlement.

The Ute woman who had walked into town from the east, following her shadow along the rutted trail, looked to be about 35 years old. She was well into middle age by the standards of the Indians. She had two young children with her. They were boys, one about four and the other a little younger, and they were stepping out manfully in the morning sun. Nobody knew whether she was the mother of one or both of the children, or a grandmother, or an aunt or just a friend. Nobody ever found out.

It was not unusual for Indians to rape their white captives. It was their right to take them, as they were simply spoils of war. It was rare that a white woman would be butchered. Normally they would be taken into the tribe, and if they worked, they were accepted. If they chose to try and escape or refused to do their share, then the chances were that they would be killed.

The taking of the Ute squaw wasn't like that. It was an act of brutal revenge for the whole town. She was grabbed and stripped. One of the women cut her simple clothes off of her with some dressmaking shears. Several times she drew blood from the naked flesh. It was as though a blind madness had gripped everyone. Even respectable women like Mrs. Hart stood and watched and whooped the men on. The children all gathered round, spitting and throwing pebbles at the screaming squaw. The Ute had no idea at all what was going on. She had no clue as to why she was being treated in this way. The word of the killings wouldn't have reached her reservation, and there was no reason for her not to come in to buy some essential provisions.

In his rage Cuchillo had gone quickly through the house, hoping to find a long gun so that he could kill some of the whites. But the Hart house was without weapons, except for a battered and dirty shotgun propped behind the kitchen door. He checked and found that it was loaded, but he thought it could be dangerous to anyone standing at either end if it were fired. From the look of the rusty muzzles and actions, it had been standing out in the garden, stock-deep in earth, for months.

When he climbed back into the attic, Cuchillo's blind anger had cooled a little. He realized that there was nothing he could do alone to rescue the woman. And even if he had been able to kill a couple of the town's folk, the smoke from a gun would have meant their locating him instantly. He'd have been trapped in the attic, and, in time, they would certainly have taken him.

The mass rape was under way as he looked down again. Cuchillo's face was set as though it were carved from the cold stone of the high Sierras.

The Indian woman was quieter, lying with her legs spread wide, arms stretched out above her head. She was trapped there by two men, one kneeling at each ankle. Another was standing with his boot heel grinding into her palm to hold her still. Cuchillo was further sickened to see that her other hand was similarly held by a woman who was looking as respectable as if she were on her way to a riverside meeting or a barn raising. Her face was lighted with an unholy glee as she smiled down at the tortured eyes of the Ute woman.

Man after man was taking the squaw. They were standing in line as if they were waiting to order a drink at the saloon, some rejoining the end of the row. One or two became impatient with the delay and knelt to use the woman in other ways.

And all the time there was a hum of chatter and cheering at the sight. Some of the whores had waked up at the two brothels of Jane and Theresa Harknett and were now on the edge of the ring of onlookers, calling out obscene advice to the men.

Gradually, the line grew shorter. More and more men were leaving to go into the saloon, out of the heat of the morning sun. Frank Bennett remained watching, hand on the butt of his pistol, striding up and down like a general at the review of his troops. He was patting each man on the back as he finished. Twice, he kicked the woman in the ribs when she seemed to slide into unconsciousness, and then he'd send a little girl for water to revive her.

"He will be the first," promised Cuchillo.

It was over. Urged on by Bennett, the last of the men, even before he'd buttoned up his breeches, slit the woman's neck with a short-bladed knife from his belt. Blood jetted out in a crimson fountain. Slowly and finally the pumping stopped as the Ute squaw died.

There was a muffled cheer that reached the ears of the grim watcher in the attic of the Hart house, and he jerked himself from the window almost as though he'd been sleeping. He turned away. The widow was back in her home; he'd heard the door slam shut and now heard her merry singing as she belatedly got herself dressed. Cuchillo wondered whether Mr. Bennett would come calling on his elderly ladylove.

He hoped so. Very much.

It sounded as if widow Hart was suffering from a bad chest. The singing was interrupted by coughing, and he heard her go into the bedroom. Then there was the sound of her gargling. Cuchillo decided that it was as good a time as any to make his move. Already he'd decided on his plan of action. He'd kill Bennett if he showed up at the house. Then he'd break for the country outside town and return after dark to carry out the last stages of his scheme of revenge.

Apart from Bennett, there were other names on Cuchillo's mental list. Albie Chesterman, Hoss Feathers and Sheldon Green were right at the top. In the scenes of vicious cruelty that trio had been the leaders.

The Apache took a moment to wonder what Thaddeus Mann would think about the extra killing when townspeople released him from the jail. Would Mann still think he'd done the right thing?

It was one thing to allow yourself to be locked in your own jail while a couple of drunken killers got what was coming to them. It was another if the blood lust spilled over to include an innocent woman and two little children.

It was the murdered children that finally and irrevocably doomed Pine's Peak. The youngest of the Indian boys had died first. He'd been picked up by his feet by the towering Albie, who giggled as he dashed the boy's skull apart on the boardwalk in front of the sheriff's own office. Blood and brains splattered in a great puddled arc of death.

Sheldon and Hoss watched and cheered the infanticide. They had then grabbed the other Ute child, all the while ignoring his terrified bawling. Sheldon took his arms, and Hoss is legs. With a three-two-one-

105

heave the deputies hurled the child high into the air, whooping as the Indian boy sprawled unconscious in the street. They did it again. On the third throw they tossed him on the roof of the dry-goods store along the jail where he hung for a long moment before rolling down the shingles and cracking dead on the planks below.

"It is enough," Cuchillo had said.

Valerie Hart, despite her sore throat, was happier than she'd been for many a long day. There hadn't been such fun in Pine's Peak since they'd caught a nigra spying on a couple of white teenage girls round the side of the livery stable way back in . . . must have been just before the great War. That had been good. But not so fine as this one. Two men, then the woman, and then those two little boys. Well, widow Hart wasn't quite sure about the children, though they had been murdering savages in the making, just like that tall Chesterman boy had shouted out.

She tried to sing another verse of "Shall We Gather at the River," but changed it halfway through to "Amazing Grace." She stopped when a bout of coughing checked her. Mr. Bennett had whispered that he might look in for a small glass of a refreshing cordial before lunch. She was minded to offer him a meal if he called. He'd been so strong and manly out there, taking charge of folks and telling them to stand in line.

Perhaps . . . her heart fluttered at the idea . . . perhaps she might show herself more open to the kind of propositions he'd been putting to her with regular enthusiasm ever since dear Henry passed on. The late Mr. Hart had left her extremely comfortably off, it must be said, a fact that counted high with the money-minded ex-banker Bennett.

Cuchillo crept slowly from the attic. His face bore an expression of cold anger that would have chilled the heart of anyone seeing him.

His eyes were cold as ice on a black-March branch; they glittered in the planes of his skull. His lips were peeled back from his even teeth in a feral snarl of hatred. Hatred. It was something that Cuchillo Oro had not felt for some time. There had been anger and revenge coursing through him for many years, but not this fresh hatred. It lay cold and bitter like frozen iron on the tongue.

The woman of the house would be the first to suffer. She had been there, encouraging the others. It was only saddening that the older man, Bennett, was not here to die with her.

As Cuchillo made his way down the stairs, one of the treads creaked underfoot. It was only a slight sound, but it carried to the ears of the widow, who was busy in the cupboard beneath the stairs, taking out her best brandy to welcome banker Bennett. She had already decided that she would flirt a little with her beau. It might add more spice to an already exciting day. Then came the creak of the stairs.

Valerie Hart knew that step well. It had creaked as long as she'd lived in the house, and she'd always meant to do something about it. Blank panic came fluttering into her mind at the sound. The third Indian—another Ute, was he? And he might be in her house, stalking down to kill her. Rape her. Possess her and make her do things that . . . For a crazed moment a wave of sexual excitement swept over her, a feeling so strong that it overwhelmed the fear, and she felt herself grow instantly moist between her thighs. Then terror reasserted itself, and she reached out and tugged the door of the cupboard closed, shutting herself into the darkness. She pressed both skinny hands to her bosom, trying to check the pounding of her heart.

Cuchillo reached the end of the stairs and paused, looking around the bottom floor, wondering where the woman had gone. Ideally, he wanted to take her as quietly as possible. A scream now could trap him in the town with too many men already breathing fast with the killing lust.

Widow Hart was aware of the tickle in her chest and the pain of wanting to cough. There was the slightest crack in the door, and she caught a glimpse of movement. A tall shadow passed by and moved into the kitchen. She closed her eyes and fought against the desire to give in to the cough. She put her head down and tried to remember a prayer to patter for her salvation. She hoped that Frank might come and kill the Indian. He'd do it. Frank would do it. Please, God, let Frank come!

Cuchillo was puzzled. He was sure that he'd have heard if the woman had left the house. Perhaps she was up on the next floor? Or maybe she was in one of the other rooms at the front of the house. The golden knife was unsheathed and in his left hand; the pale light reflected off it, dancing in the mirror in the hallway. He went past the cupboard under the stairs, never giving it a second glance. And, with her eyes tightly closed, Valerie Hart never saw him pass. She thought he was in the kitchen, or prayed that he might have left the house through the back door.

The parlor was filled with furniture—overfilled, some might say. Sofas and chairs jostled each other for the limited space; small ornaments of china and glass elbowed for room on the sideboard. Cuchillo paused and stared around, wondering whether she might be cowering in the far corner by the pianola. He eased himself silently across to check.

In the blackness the Widow Hart had lost her nerve. All sense of time had abandoned her, and she wasn't sure whether she'd been hiding for a minute or an hour, or more or less. With a low moan she pushed the door open and scampered out into the hall. Not looking back, she slithered into the kitchen, her staring eyes caught by the sight of the battered old scattergun.

"Yes. Oh, Blessed Jesus Christ Almighty! Thank you. Oh, thank you, God!" She picked it up and cocked both hammers, ignoring the rust and mud and filth that clogged it.

Cuchillo heard her and turned. He flattened himself against the wall of the parlor and slowly peered around the corner of the hall. He saw the woman, jacketed in bombazine black, holding the shotgun, her back to him. She was looking out into the garden.

Mrs. Hart was befuddled. She wasn't sure whether to lock the house and risk shutting herself in with the Ute warrior, or to go out into the open air and then have the hazard that he might be out there waiting for her to do just that. Perhaps she should go out by the front door.

As she spun around, Cuchillo pulled back into the silent room, out of her sight. He heard the woman click a few steps toward the front of the hall, then stop again.

It was at that moment that Frank Bennett, with whiskey on his breath and blood on his hands, came around the back of the house and walked confidently up to the kitchen door.

He had less than one minute to live.

A whole lot less.

CHAPTER TWELVE

Panic was riding high on the shoulders of Valerie Hart, blanking her mind to all reason and sense. She knew that the scattergun had been neglected for years; she could even see the red rust staining her fingers like powdered blood as she gripped the dusty stock. But that didn't mean a thing. All that mattered was that there was the awful, murdering savage around, after her. He wasn't after anyone else in Pine's Peak—just *her!*

Banker Bennett, as he liked to be called, took off his smart gray hat, holding the brim in his right hand. His mind was vaguely on Mrs. Hart and her money. And she was still a damned pretty filly, he thought. Over the last months there had been a few debts building up from his love of blackjack. Ed Droodle, owner of the saloon, wasn't a kindly man over gambling debts; he had been dropping hints about knees getting broken in accidents. Bennett didn't cotton much to the idea of that sort of accident happening to him.

111

He stepped up and raised his fist to knock smartly on the glass-paneled door.

And then he died.

Widow Hart heard the noise of feet and spun around. She saw the dim figure, the outline visible as a black, haunting shape through the patterned window above the kitchen door.

"No!" she called, her voice strangled in her throat so that it came out as a whisper that barely shook the beams of dusty sunlight darting across the room. Her finger tightened on the first trigger of the gun. She braced her hip against the stock. The kick nearly toppled her off her feet.

The gun went off with a boom, and the house filled with a cloud of foul powder smoke. The shot sprayed out from the end of the barrel after clearing out the clogged mud on the way. It burst across the kitchen and smashed the glass.

Frank Bennett died puzzled, wondering what it was that broke the door in his face. His last coherent thought was that it was a fist. Someone had somehow been hiding and had punched him in the mouth. That was why he was aware of hurtling backward. His eyes hurt. He couldn't see. His mouth was filled with blood and broken sharp bits of bone. The lead hit him full in the face, coming close to taking his head clean off his shoulders, flaying the skin from his skull, peeling away his lips and nose, pulping his eyes.

It took him about ten seconds to realize that he might be badly hurt. By the time he got around to wondering just how badly he was hurt, it was too late, and he was a warm corpse out in the Colorado sun.

Mrs. Hart didn't realize that. All she knew was that the enemy out back had been hit. She'd seen that much before she nearly fell. She clutched the gun and wondered whether to run and see what she'd done, safe in the knowledge that she had a second barrel to use if the damned Indian wasn't dead yet.

Cuchillo could almost reach out and touch her, but he was temporarily confused. From where he was hiding, he hadn't seen or heard the arrival of Frank Bennett. He'd just heard the boom of the heavy gun and the crashing of the door splintering under the shot. He assumed that she'd somehow spotted him, and he winced at the sudden explosion, flattening himself against the wall, turning his head away. But there was no pain. By peeking around the edge of the door, he saw her staring into the kitchen.

The tall Apache was so bewildered that his reflexes lost their razor edge, and he was caught flat-footed when the widow spun around and saw him— less than 15 feet away.

"Blessed Jesus! Another," she said in a calm, conversational tone, as if she were handing around the cakes at a church social. Cuchillo stood there, trapped in the doorway of the parlor, and watched as she lifted the heavy gun to her shoulder. She pressed her face against the walnut butt, closed by the rusted action. She was squinting at him, her finger ready on the second trigger.

A tiny segment of time seemed to break off and

hang suspended in the air while the Apache and the elderly white woman looked at each other. Cuchillo knew he didn't have a chance unless she could be persuaded not to pull the trigger and blow him away. Any sudden movement from him, and she'd surely kill him.

Widow Hart was undecided. It was good to have the big buck in her power, and for a moment she wished that Frank would hurry up to see her success. One Indian was dead out back, and another one was at her mercy inside. What the women of her quilting circle would say when they heard about it! The chatter and the praise, it made her cheeks blush at the thought.

Cuchillo didn't move a muscle, though his mind was racing. That shot must have been heard outside, and within a few seconds someone was going to be running in to catch him. If he could just risk an underarm throw of the golden cinqueda. . . .

Valerie Hart saw the flicker of movement in the eyes of the Apache, and all her earlier panic came rushing back. Without any conscious effort on her part, the index finger of her right hand crooked itself harder around the narrow trigger of the scattergun, and she fired the charge in the second barrel.

Cuchillo's mind worked faster than most men's, but even he was surprised at what happened. He stood frozen to the carpet of the trim parlor as blood and brains and shards of bone splattered all around him, staining his shirt and breeches. Flesh and torn gristle dappled the floor around his feet. And no part of that carnage was his.

During the time that the shotgun had been neglected, left out in winter storms and mud, small stones had become lodged in the barrels, and then more dirt rammed in on top. The first barrel had just about blown clean on through, but the second charge didn't make it. Unable to burst out of the muzzle, the lead found an alternative route from the gun. It flew out the side, blowing the breech apart right by the Widow Hart's tender face.

Her dying was quicker and more merciful than her mean and petty nature merited.

The corpse was blown against the wall and lay kicking in the hall. Smoking remains of the burst weapon were at her side. Both hands clawed at where her face had been, as though they were determined to prove that nothing had happened. Her hands touched the sodden, broken cheeks, exploring where her eyes had been, twitching in what was a macabre reflex.

Cuchillo looked down at the body of the old woman, grinning nervously at his own fortune. He wondered how long it would be before someone arrived to investigate the noise.

"I say that there is no hope for woman who loses her head," he said to himself, stepping quickly over the body and peering out of the back door. He then saw the shambles that had once been Banker Bennett. Cuchillo stooped and took the dead man's pistol from its holster and then ran silently into the garden.

Sheldon Green was unlucky. There was so much noise going on in the saloon, with all the good old boys gathering around to celebrate the rape and the lynchings, that nobody there had heard the sound of the two gunshots—nobody but Sheldon.

He'd been out back, down near the small stream, using the rickety privy with the door that had to be held shut. Someone a year or so ago had tried to cut shapes in the woodwork—a club, a diamond, a heart and a spade—but they'd been drunk first and clumsy second, and all that was there to show were four irregular holes that let in flies in the summer and snow in the winter.

Sheldon had been sitting quietly, his breeches around his ankles, weeping to himself for his dead twin.

"Sure I hated him, Lord, but that didn't mean you had to go and fuckin' have him killed by that fuckin' Indian! That just weren't plain fair."

That was when he heard the distant sound of the shotgun. In a contest for brains, Sheldon Green could have been given a head start by the average fence post and still come in second, but he recognized gunfire when he heard it. He'd already tugged up his pants and was buckling his belt when he recalled an omission.

"Shit!" he exclaimed, giggling as he realized that he'd made a kind of joke. He dropped his breeches again and remedied the damage to his combinations as best he could with a couple sheets of the mail-order catalog that hung on a rusting nail on the wall of the privy.

Just as he was pulling them up for the second time, he heard the distant rumble of another shot, which was more muffled than the first. Sheldon guessed that it was probably a couple of the men celebrating the good day that Pine's Peak was enjoying; so he didn't hurry.

As he came out, he looked up and down the street, but nothing seemed to have happened. There were no signs of anyone rushing around. He wiped the remnants of tears from his eyes and started back toward the saloon. He decided that he'd go down the alley at the side and maybe look in on the sheriff. Nobody had dared to go and see Thaddeus Mann after the way happenings had gotten themselves a mite out of hand. People figured that his notorious temper might get the better of him. But Sheldon was too dim to think about that, and he started across the street.

He saw Cuchillo Oro just at the moment the big Apache was breaking for cover. The Indian had decided to take a chance on making it to the brush and woodland out beyond the township, toward the remnants of the old railroad.

"Hey! Hey, you!" Sheldon called, drawing his pistol, trying to make his mind up what he ought to be doing. The sheriff would have known, but he was locked safely away in his own jail. And the rest of the boys were in the saloon having themselves a shit-kicking good time. That left him.

Cuchillo saw the deputy draw his pistol, and he stood his ground for a moment, weighing up the odds. He'd seen something of the surviving twin while in the jail, and he'd been impressed by Sheldon's stupidity. The fact that he hadn't even fired a shot to bring help was a fair enough token of that.

"You stand still there, you 'pache bastard!"

117

shouted Green, but his voice wasn't loud enough to carry to the rest of the town.

Cuchillo allowed his shoulders to droop as though he was in despair at being so easily caught. His left hand with Bennett's pistol in it was behind his back; his mutilated right hand was stretched out as though he were begging for mercy.

Green ran across the street, nearly turning his ankle as a boot heel caught in a rut. His face was showing a wet-lipped grin at the thought of what a hero he'd be. Mann'd be pleased with him. Maybe the sheriff would forget how some things had gone a mite too far with the woman and her brats.

"Do not shoot me!" called the Apache, glancing sideways to make sure that Bennett's body was clearly visible to anyone coming into the garden of the late Widow Hart. It was there all right, spread-eagled in a great gleaming pool of bright blood, unrecognizable because of the devastating injuries to the head.

Sheldon Green ran in through the gate. He'd ducked under the clothesline and came to a skidding halt about six feet from Cuchillo. He'd never even considered in his excitement that the tall warrior might be holding a gun in his hidden hand.

"Now I got you and . . ."

Cuchillo slowly pointed down to the left, behind the dusty flower bed, close by the shattered back door of the neat little house.

"You must think I'm dumb to fall for an old trick like . . . like that . . . Holy Jesus! Who's . . . ?"

His eyes started out from their sockets, like the stops on a mission harmonium, as he saw the torn

118

corpse. The gun drooped in his hand from the shock. From the gray suit he figured that it had to be Banker Bennett, but he couldn't imagine what devastating accident had happened to him. The head looked like an anvil had fallen on it from a third story.

Cuchillo stepped in very close. The remains of his right hand gripped Green's wrist and twisted it hard so that the pistol fell into the dirt. The barrel of his own gun was jammed deep into the deputy's guts, making him nearly double over as he fought for breath.

"Mister . . . don't . . ."

There wasn't time for any big speeches, because Cuchillo wanted to be safe away from the center of the township. Bennett's gun held six rounds of ammunition, and the Apache worked the double action of the heavy Tranter three times. He held the body upright as it jerked from the devastating kick of the bullets. Sheldon Green's fat belly absorbed most of the sound of the gun, muffling the explosions.

Finally, Cuchillo let him fall. He bent over to pick up the dying boy's own pistol, tucking it in his belt alongside the half-empty Tranter. Green moaned and pressed his hands to the scorched front of his shirt where the single black hole was leaking a surprisingly small amount of blood.

"It will be a long passing for you," said Cuchillo. "There will be time enough for you to think of what you have done this day and many days before it."

Sheriff Thaddeus Mann had gotten over his anger. The cell he was in had blocked him off from much of what had happened, but he was an experienced lawman, and he knew what a lynch mob sounded like. The wind had been in the right direction for the stench of scorched flesh to reach his nostrils. Then he had listened, his knuckles white on the bars, as the Ute woman was raped and killed, and the children brutally murdered. The shouts and jeers of the crowd had given him the clues as to what had been going on. He'd also heard the two shots from the scattergun. And he'd even caught the faint sound of Sheldon Green's death wounds.

His lips shaped the words "Cuchillo Oro," and he wondered how long it would be before the good folks of Pine's Peak came shamefaced to release him. By then he suspected that the big Apache would be long miles off, beyond his reach.

It was an understandable thing for him to have thought, but Sheriff Mann was utterly, disasterously wrong.

CHAPTER THIRTEEN

Had it not been for the mindless level of violence that Cuchillo Oro had been forced to witness, he would have run from Pine's Peak and carried on running, and there wasn't a man in the settlement that would have caught him. Maybe the wily Thaddeus Mann could have come close, but even he would have given best to the Apache with the sort of start that Cuchillo had stolen for himself.

But that was the whole point. He wasn't going to run any farther than the railroad tunnel where Crooked Eye and Wounded Bear had been trapped. That would do for a hideout until darkness again cloaked the land.

They let Thaddeus Mann out of his own jail a little before dusk, having drawn lots to see who got the job of unlocking the cell. It was Ed Droodle who drew the short straw. He had simply eased open the door of the office and lobbed the keys in so that the sheriff could reach them through the bars. By the time Mann came out into the street, it was virtually deserted but for a handful of older women who were standing grouped together for comfort and courage, huddled like fowl when they see the shadow of the chicken hawk.

It was Abigail O'Connor, frail and trembling, her voice constantly on the edge of tears, who told Mann about what had been happening—about the three new corpses in Pine's Peak and how they'd been found.

The lawman didn't say anything. He only nodded courteously as she finished the tale of disaster, and plucked at the brim of his hat. Then he stalked away down the street. When one of the women roused enough courage to ask him where he was going, he turned around with a faint look of surprise on his face.

"Home, Miss Gordon. I'm going on home to do me some thinking." He stopped and then turned back again. "And tell folks I'd take it mighty kindly if'n they'd all keep indoors and out of my sight."

Jimmy Reisner's gun shop stood near the edge of the settlement, not far from where the railroad lines would have run. After the horrors of the day Jimmy was sitting, drinking, looking back on what had happened and wondering what had turned decent folks into animals. After the deaths of the widow, the banker and the deputy had been discovered, panic set in damn quickly, with women dragging screaming children along by their pinafores to safety. Doors were slammed and bolts slid across. Men loaded up their guns and made sure their horses were locked up for the night. There was even talk of sending a galloper after the Cavalry, with fears of the Utes rising and slaughtering them all in their beds.

As far as that went, Jimmy Reisner had lived long enough around Pine's Peak to be confident that the Indians wouldn't dare band together against the township. They were too cowed and beaten. But this Apache that he'd heard about sounded like something different. The gunsmith's stock of rifles and ammunition were safe enough. The door from the outside was set with iron bars to brace it, and the weapons were all in a separate cupboard that was chained and padlocked.

Before going to his bed, Jimmy looked at his precious guns, wondering whether he ought to take them down to the jail for extra protection. That would have meant facing Sheriff Thaddeus Mann, and he didn't rightly fancy that very much. Maybe if he just took the long guns—specially the 50-caliber Sharps buffalo gun with the special hunting sight on it. It was a powerful gun, capable of hitting and killing a man at a half mile in good conditions in the hands of a top marksman. Even in the hands of an average marksman the Sharps would kill nine shots from ten at 200 paces. It was about the finest gun that Jimmy Reisner had seen in a long while. It had been a special order, paid for in advance, by a local man who'd then died of a consumption the previous winter while waiting for delivery of the rifle.

In the end Jimmy left the Sharps where it was and went up early to bed, nursing a headache and a pint of whiskey. He slept fairly well, though dreams plagued him. He had nightmares of bands of hostile

Apaches who were stripped and painted for war, raiding his store, taking all of his guns and mocking him. In the dream it seemed to Reisner that his feet were caught in molasses and he couldn't move to stop the Indians from their robbery. They leaped and chanted, poking at him with long spears and beating on the walls with great clubs. The banging and crashing went on and on, until it woke him and he sat up straight in his bed, his head pounding from the liquor, his whole body soaked in sweat. The banging had been so real.

"Goddamned real," he muttered.

The throbbing in his temples was so severe that he decided to go down and get himself a drink of water from the crock in the kitchen. His nightdress flapped against his bare calves as he went sleepily down the stairs, steadying himself against the rough wall. He paused at the bottom and noticed that he'd left the lamp on in the room with the guns. Blinking and shaking his head at such absent-mindedness, he pushed the door open and took three steps into the pool of yellow light.

Cuchillo Oro shot him twice. The second bullet was insurance, because the first round took the gunsmith through the middle of his face, killing him instantly, toppling him backward. The second bullet hit him through the throat as he fell. It passed through him and tore out a chunk of white wood from the frame of the door.

Jimmy Reisner died wondering whether this was still part of the same dream about Apaches robbing him of his guns. There *was* a tall Apache with ruthless and chilling eyes, and there were his guns, the chain ripped from the wall, the rifles and carbines scattered about the floor. It was a double-action Tranter that killed him. Jimmy noticed that it looked like Banker Bennett's handgun. There was even time for that much before he was killed.

The Tranter was now useless to the Apache; so he dropped it and selected instead a pair of matched Colts with fancy butts and engraved chambers, which Reisner had been keeping in the hope of finding a special customer for them. But in the slowly dying town of Pine's Peak he'd more or less given up on them.

Apart from the pistols and 40 rounds of ammunition, Cuchillo also filled a small pack with some blasting powder and 50 rounds of ammunition for the Sharps. There was a selection of straps on the wall, and he took one, buckling the heavy rifle across his shoulders.

He looked quickly around the gun shop to see if there was anything else that he needed to aid his revenge on the settlement. But he decided that there was nothing more to be done. Cuchillo resisted the temptation to set fire to the store, not wanting to give a premature warning of his plans. The decent folk of Pine's Peak would all know soon enough.

The two old Utes had told Cuchillo something about the town. He knew where the food and liquor were stored, and for a few moments the Apache had considered indulging his liking for the firewater of the whites. But there was something else kept in one of the big outhouses back of the main street that interested him more.

Moving quietly as a panther in the night, Cuchillo worked his way along from the railroad tunnel into Pine's Peak. The town was quiet, the saloon and brothels closed and shuttered. Every house that the Apache walked past was dark, the drapes drawn tight. The killings of the day had produced an odd effect; the heady excitement of the bloody violence had been replaced by shame and a dull sickness in most of the townspeople's minds. Many of them prayed before going early to their beds that night. They prayed on their knees for mercy for their sins.

It's possible that God heard them and pitied them. Cuchillo heard nothing.

Larry "Hoss" Feathers was a tall, good-looking boy who was favored by many of the single ladies of the township, and by some married women who should have known better. Larry wasn't very much into bothering about remorse over a couple of stinking old men, a Ute whore and two bawling bastards. It had been a good day, even though he was as scared as the rest over Thaddeus Mann's seething rage at what had happened. But that would pass, and things would drift back to what they were before. It would have been nice to have caught the Apache responsible for killing both the Green twins, but maybe the town would be better off if the Indian were out of Pine's Peak and long gone. He'd surely been a tall, murderin' son of a bitch, that Cuchillo Oro.

Larry had gotten himself loaded with whiskey before the saloon closed up, and he'd found one of his favorite ladies. Emily Simon was married, but she never let it bother her. Her husband, Mortimer, was a drummer. The year saw him cover a couple-thousand miles, by train, from Montana across to Vermont and back into Oregon. That left Emily on her own for long, long months, and she was happy to scratch her own special itch with a sporting boy like Larry Feathers.

They'd gone out back together at around 8 o'clock that evening, taking some bread and meat and a bottle of liquor with them. They had found their favorite quiet place behind the store. There was a covered lean-to with a pile of old mattresses in it. It was just snug and right for some secret loving.

At a little after 11 o'clock they both fell asleep, worn out with the excitement and the drink and the strenuous coupling. She was naked, with only a blanket they'd brought with them across the lower part of her body. Larry kept his shirt on, with his boots and breeches hung neatly over a nail. The gun belt was hanging alongside.

Emily was deeply asleep, snoring a little, mouth sagging open. Her left hand was under the blanket and hanging on to Larry's considerable weapon. A half-smile was on her lips as her lusts reached snaking into her dreams.

Cuchillo killed her with his golden knife. With unmovable pressure he pressed the palm of his own crippled hand over her mouth, dislocating her jaw with his strength. The golden cinqueda in his left hand drove in under her left breast and sliced through the walls of her heart. He held her still as she tried to fight her way free of him, legs kicking off the blanket, eyes bursting open with terror. She died quickly, though the releases of fear made her foul herself.

Her death hardly disturbed Larry Feathers. He was only aware of his mistress's fingers as they tightened convulsively about his penis, bringing him immediately to full erection. Hoss might not have been great shakes as a deputy sheriff, but he was a lively and always-dependable stud. There was a slight coolness about his loins, as though someone had lifted off the blanket, and he grunted a sleepy protest.

The boy's swollen manhood, white in the glittering moonlight, was too fine a target for Cuchillo to resist. Gripping the great knife firmly in his left hand, the big Apache held it across his own chest. His eyes were impassive as he made a vicious, sweeping slash downward. He severed Larry's pride and joy in one savage cut near the root where the tendrils of wiry hair curled about at the base of his stomach.

The blood pumped out with such force that it splashed on the opposite wall of the lean-to, fully six feet from the ground, black in the night. Fully awake, Feathers tried to scream out as his hand went to the ghastly wound. But Cuchillo was ready for that. As the deputy's mouth cracked wide open, he knifed him. The broad, triangular blade jammed in between the uneven teeth and cut partway through the tongue. The tip of the knife jammed between the bones of the spine. The Apache's fist pushed Feathers flat on his back and held him still, pressed into the comfortable softness of the mattresses. Cuchillo kept him there until the boy was dead.

There had been special reasons for killing the young deputies, and Cuchillo was glad that he had managed to take three out of the four, with only the skinny Albie Chesterman left alive. And with much of the night remaining, there was more than a chance that he might take him as well.

The next steps involved getting into the main storage hut by levering off the bolts that held it locked. Then for the next two hours Cuchillo Oro worked furiously hard, dragging here and there, making sure that everything would be ready. He was using some of the blasting powder that he'd taken from the gunsmith's, and he was setting fuses. The stink of the heavy oil that now soaked around most of the main buildings of Pine's Peak hung in the air, but the town was sleeping, and nobody noticed that their doom was close upon them.

At last, carrying the Sharps and the pistols, the Apache was ready to carry out the final, dreadful act of his revenge. He lit the end of the first of many fuses, and he watched the glittering red worm of fire as it hissed across the ground.

"Now," he said. "Now it begins."

CHAPTER FOURTEEN

"Bring up the twelve-pounders!"

"All the mules are dead here, Sir!"

Captain Thaddeus Mann was asleep, fighting again and again the War that had left him emotionally crippled so many years back.

It might have been Manassas or Wilderness or bloody Shiloh. Mann could never tell. When he was locked in his dreams, he fought in a blind fog of death and ruin, a fog peopled by shadows of men he'd known.

"Thaddeus. Stop the noise," said a woman's voice at his elbow. She was a pretty woman. Her face was shaded by a large-brimmed white hat with fresh red roses around the edges. Dew was hanging on each perfect petal.

"Rachel, go home. There's too much . . ." He couldn't think of the word he wanted. Then it came. ". . . dying. Too much dying."

"I can no longer be hurt by that, for I am long with the spirits of the other world, my beloved," she replied, smiling up at him so gently that he feared his heart would burst.

"Then go by the lake in that white building yonder," he said and then ducked as a shell came whining in overhead. Perhaps it was Chancellorsville. But there hadn't been a lake at Chancellorsville.

"I will wait for you, Thaddeus, forever if I must," she replied, kissing him on the cheek. Her kiss was like the fleeting touch of a falling leaf. But the touch was cold as ice, and he shivered.

There was a man standing in the shadows, waiting for him as he turned from watching his wife walk quickly toward safety. The man was a tall soldier in dusty blue carrying a .577 Enfield rifle musket. The bayonet was glittering in the misty sunlight. Or was it a knife fixed there? It seemed to have the warm glow of gold.

Thaddeus Mann turned and walked toward the specter. Then he started to run, faster and faster. The Union private stepped out from the shadows, and the captain saw that he wasn't white. The soldier was an Apache with long, braided hair tied back off his shoulders. And it *was* a knife.

A golden knife.

"Noooo!" screamed Mann as he turned and tried to escape from the vengeful ghost. It was coming after him in long, slow, threatening strides, eating up the ground. If he could reach the safety of the white house by the lake. . . .

"Hurry, my dearest!" called the woman, who was waiting for him. Her long dress was blowing across her body in the rising wind, and one hand was holding the white hat on her head. "Hurry, Thaddeus!"

Then there was smoke. It was wreathing about the wood-framed house, shrouding his wife from sight with the red glow of flames. Thaddeus Mann wanted to stop running and go for help, but he could hear the soldier at his heels. He could almost feel the sharp pain of the golden knife slicing between his ribs.

The fire was gaining hold, and he could even see the bottom of the white dress charring and falling into ashes. He watched as the red roses wilted and tumbled from the hat. A gust of wind came, and he saw Rachel's hair catch fire like a great halo, and yet she didn't move. She just stood and watched him run for his life with that same patient smile that she had always worn.

"Rachel! Rachel!" he screamed, feeling the breath catching in his lungs, tasting the bitterness of smoke that made it hard to breathe.

There was yelling, and he heard cries for help and the sharp crackle of musket fire. And above it all he was conscious of the smoke.

Sheriff Thaddeus Mann of Pine's Peak, Colorado Territory, woke at a little before 3 o'clock in the morning.

He could hear yells and cries for help and the distant crack of a powerful rifle.

And above it all he was conscious of the smoke.

It had been easy for Cuchillo Oro to set fire to the town. The wind had been veering northerly, and a little after midnight it began to rise until it had reached a stiff breeze. The fuses of powder were

133

then lit, and they, in turn, ignited the oil-sodden wood of the houses and stores of the township. By laying the trails and preparing the ground well, the Apache had made sure that several of the fires would begin simultaneously, with others springing up only moments later.

By the time the folks started to wake up to the realization of the burning, it was too late to save their homes. The flames were already roaring up, licking at the shingled roofs, blistering paint off windows and doors. Barns were blazing from end to end, and the air was heavy with the terrified screams of trapped animals.

Some of them started to try and fight the flames, but it was impossible. The wind was blowing crimson ashes all around, and dozens of new fires were starting in the dry brush around the settlement. It didn't take long for real panic to set in. Men began throwing their possessions out into the street where women in night clothes were hugging their bawling children.

Warnings were being shouted, and the old and infirm were being helped from their burning dwellings to stand huddled or to lie on piles of blankets amid the smoke and rain of cinders.

Josiah Cooperstown lived with his elderly father and unmarried sister in one of the last houses, nearly next-door to Sheriff Mann. He woke to the barking of his sister's pet dog and found that the whole eastern end of his house was hopelessly ablaze. Flames were soaring to the roof. The fire was rushing along the floor, snaking along from room to room.

Fighting off panic, Josiah managed to rouse his father, who was convinced that either the dam had burst or that Nathan Bedford Forrest had come for him. But he wandered quietly enough outside where Josiah's sister was waiting for him. While they stood in the bright light of the fire, seeing that the whole town was ablaze, Josiah went back in to try and salvage what possessions he could. He was particularly proud of his collection of English books, and he grabbed armfuls of them and threw them out on the grass as carefully as possible.

His sister, Carrie, was trying to help him while keeping a worried eye on their father, who was standing shivering and looking at the town. He was muttering about the night they burned Dixie down. When Josiah appeared again at a window, smoke was billowing about him. He called out to Carrie to take some more of his beloved books while he went back for more.

She was only six feet away from him when she heard a strange sound, like a hornet buzzing past her ears. And then Josiah vanished, kicked back into the house. All she had seen was the blooming of a scarlet spider, which was hanging there in the center of her brother's head, as a 50-caliber bullet hit him between the eyes.

Her scream was lost amid the general noise from the rest of the good people of Pine's Peak.

Cuchillo had once been to a county fair about three years back, somewhere up north in the Dakotas. And there had been a side-show attraction involving a large cask filled with water. There had been about 30 or 40 smallish fish swimming around in it. The sign said, "Easy as shooting fish in a barrel!" Five dollars would be given to anyone who could shoot and kill one of the creatures using an ordinary handgun. Many had tried, but none of them had succeeded. The wily fish had learned to keep in the bottom half of the barrel, and the water was deep enough to slow up the bullets, even if you allowed for the difficulties of aiming off to compensate for the refraction of the water.

Compared to shooting those fish at the county fair, killing the decent men of Pine's Peak was ridiculously easy. The fires gave a wonderful light to shoot by, and the Sharps handled sweet and easy. Cuchillo dodged around in the brush, avoiding the burning patches, picking his targets and gunning them down. His first nine shots killed eight men and wounded another so that he fell and rolled and screamed.

The tenth bullet killed him as well.

The Apache took care not to shoot any of the women or young children. He also avoided the distinctive gray-haired figure of Sheriff Mann when he came running along, buckling on his gun belt. Mann stopped and stood stricken in the middle of what had once been his town.

"It's that bitchin' Cuchillo Oro!" he shouted. His words were clearly audible to the hiding Indian.

To prove Mann right, Cuchillo neatly put a 50-caliber shot through the chest of the man the sheriff had been talking to, knocking him over in the dirt. He coughed up blood at the lawman's feet.

"Get everyone out of town! Everyone! Come on, or he'll butcher every mother-lovin' man here!"

"Get after him! He can't do this!" shrieked an elderly woman whose mobcap was hanging lopsided on her straggling, thin gray locks.

"Guess not, but he is!" yelled Sheriff Mann.

"Why?" yelped a young man who Cuchillo recognized as being one of the first to take his place in line for seconds at the Ute squaw, and who had cheered on the deputies as they murdered the young children.

"Because I figure he is a whole lot sicker than me about what you folks done yesterday, and I can't . . ."

There was another crack of the Sharps, and the man at the sheriff's side fell, clutching his throat, lying, feet scrabbling in the street. His shadow was bizarrely lengthened by the bright fires all around.

Mann looked down at him and shook his head. Then he finished his last sentence. ". . . and I can't say I rightly blame him all that much."

Most folks finally got out alive. A couple of men were rash enough to try and harness up their animals to wagons, but both of them died within seconds of each other. The rest realized that if they had a chance at all, it was only to leave everything they possessed and flee the town. They would have to allow the fires to blaze unchecked, to destroy all of their homes and stores, leaving Pine's Peak a charred and glowing bare patch in the land.

Nineteen men were killed by Cuchillo Oro that night, and the slow dying of the settlement was over.

CHAPTER FIFTEEN

By morning there wasn't a lot left of the township. A few of the outlying houses and homesteads had survived the conflagration, including Sheriff Mann's own place. But all of the rest had gone, tumbled into ashes. Several smoke columns rose and mingled until they formed a single, vast gray-black smudge against the soft pinkness of the dawn sky.

The people had left. The dead were still lying where they'd fallen, spread-eagled in the street or outside their homes. Two or three of the corpses, including that of Albie Chesterman, were twisted and blackened in the shells of the buildings.

Although both brothels had been closed, Albie had climbed in round back, eager to make a better acquaintance of one of the new whores, Amanda Jennings, a high yellow girl from near Baton Rouge. When she'd left him around midnight, after having sucked him dry for his three dollars, Albie had fallen asleep up on the top floor of the brothel.

And when the fires came to Pine's Peak, everyone forgot about him in the panic. By the time he woke, the whole place was ablaze. Cuchillo saw his pale, thin face appear suddenly at a window, but the crashing of glass was inaudible in the general noise. The flames had come up the central stairs of the bordello, and the tall deputy was trapped.

Sheriff Mann stood and watched from the street as Albie made a try for his life. He climbed out through the window and hung on by his hands to the sill. His feet were reaching desperately for the ledge of the next floor down. With his great height, Chesterman might have made it. His limbs seemed elongated and black, like a dangling spider, against the white wall of the burning building. Immediately beneath him the front porch was well ablaze, and the flames were licking almost as high as the hanging boy.

Though he was a vicious, humorless killer, Albie made a brave bid to save his skin. If it hadn't been for Cuchillo and the long buffalo rifle, he might have managed to reach safety.

The Apache put a small dab of spittle on the foresight of the Sharps to make it stand out better against the bright lights. Cuddling the stock firmly into his shoulder, he squinted along the barrel, lining it up on Albie, who was hanging free, his feet reaching for the wooden ledge that would take some of his weight. Cuchillo's finger tightened on the trigger. And gently, he squeezed it.

The bullet took Chesterman through the left wrist, pulping the bones and shattering the tendons. He screamed piercingly at the sudden agony and then tightened his grip with the right hand. Though he was only three inches short of seven feet, Albie was incredibly thin, and it was no great strain on his other hand to hold him dangling there, 25 feet above the crescendo of fire.

Thaddeus Mann looked around, staring into the cauldron of blackness that held Pine's Peak cradled at its center. He knew that Cuchillo Oro must be out there not too far away, and he looked for the muzzle flash that might give him a clue to the location of the Apache warrior. And he guessed that there would be a second bullet.

Locked into his own nightmare of heat and fumes and pain, Albie Chesterman closed his eyes and concentrated all his flagging energy on keeping his grip. He knew that if he fell, he was a dead man; he'd plunge through the burning wood of the porch to a scorching, blistering end.

Cuchillo reloaded the Sharps. And gently, he squeezed the trigger again.

Although he was looking hard, Mann missed the shot. It was lost in the whirling red points of light from the flames. All about him there was a roaring wind, which was generated by the fire storm. It sucked in the air and made it hard to breathe. But above all the noise and yelling, Mann heard the mortal cry of the last of his four deputies as he plunged to his fiery doom. His right wrist had also been torn apart by the accurately aimed bullet.

That was the last of the deaths.

Before leaving the area the next morning, Cuchillo crept from his hiding place near the ill-fated railroad and looked a last time at the remains of Pine's Peak. The people would come back to bury

141

their dead, but that would be all. Nobody would ever bother to try and rebuild the township. There wasn't any reason.

But among the blackened ruins, there was one person moving. A tall, gray-haired man, wearing a silver badge in his lapel—a badge that, even as the Apache watched him from the hillside, the sheriff took off and threw down in the trampled dirt of the main street. The morning sun flickered brightly off it. Then he straightened up and looked around. His thumbs were hooked in his gun belt.

Cuchillo had the rifle, and there was a passing temptation to gun the lawman down where he stood, but the Apache ignored it. He had a grudging respect for the white man; he saw him as being less guilty for what had happened.

And there was some depth to Mann that he recognized. He was a tough, lonely, brave man, and Cuchillo had no wish to kill him.

"Hey, Apache! Golden Knife!" called out Thaddeus Mann suddenly, his voice ringing back from the hills around.

Cuchillo didn't reply, but flattened himself in case it was a trap.

"I know you're there. I can think like you, Apache. I done some fighting in my days. I know. Know why you done this. Can understand it, son. Really can. Town was dying, and you just slammed down the coffin lid on it."

Cuchillo started to move slowly away toward the west and the high mountains. But he could still hear the voice of the elderly lawman shouting to the morning.

"You know what I got to do. I got to come after you. This was my town. Mine! You killed it and lots of folks. I got no choice. I'll hunt you down, Cuchillo Oro! You hear me? You hear me?"

The big Indian still moved on, but paused on a gaunt crag and looked back. On an impulse he drew the golden knife and turned its gleaming blade so that the sun bounced off it, catching the eye of Thaddeus Mann.

"Yeah. I see you. I see you, Cuchillo. I'll play your game, boy. Play it right on through. You got a good lead, 'cos I got me things to do. Things to do here. Knots to tie tight and doors to close for good. Then I'll come after you."

The voice became fainter as the warrior padded on ahead of the chasing sun, not bothering to look back again. But he could still hear the last words of the lawman: "It's not over, Cuchillo. Not over . . . This . . . isn't . . . the . . . end. Not . . . the . . . end."

SPECIAL PREVIEW

The blazing Western series by the author of the bestselling EDGE series

George G. Gilman

The adventures of Adam Steele are written by the author of our bestselling Edge *series, who has created another brand of blazing Westerns to show the way it really was in the West . . . a grim and gritty view unpolished by history, untamed by time!*

Outraged over his father's murder, Adam Steele rides to his destiny on a bloody trail of revenge and retribution. He carries with him a rifle bearing the dedication that is his inspiration: "To Benjamin P. Steele, with gratitude, Abraham Lincoln." And Steele won't stop until he finds his father's killers . . . and any other killer who crosses his path!

The following is an edited version of the first few chapters, as we are introduced to Adam Steele*:

Adam Steele reined his bay gelding to a halt at the crest of a rise and split his mouth in a gentle smile as he surveyed the lights of the city spread before him. It had been a long ride from Richmond and he spent a few relaxed moments in quiet contemplation of the end of the journey. Then he sighed and heeled the horse forward down the gentle incline that led into Washington.

He rode upright, but not tall in the Western saddle. He was just a shade over five feet six inches in height, his build compact rather than slight, and suggested adequate strength instead of power. Like so many young men who have survived the bitter fighting of the war just ended, he looked older than his actual years, which totaled twenty-eight. He had a long face with regular features that gave him a nondescript handsomeness. His mouthline was gentle, his nose straight, and his coal black eyes honest. His hair was prematurely gray with only a few hanks of dark red to show its former coloration. It was trimmed neat and short, and this was the only obvious sign of the five years he had spent in the army of the Confederate States.

The city was very quiet as Steele entered the streets of its southern section and he was mildly surprised at this. Washington was the capital of the victorious northern states and he had expected it still to be in the throes of triumphant revelry even this long after Lee's surrender. But he did not give too much thought to the matter, for he had another, more important subject on his mind. He had no trouble finding his way to his destination, for he had been a frequent visitor to the city in pre-war days and little had changed during the intervening years.

It was not until he turned onto Tenth Street that he pulled up short in surprise. The street was as quiet as all the others had been, but there was a difference. Where the others had been deserted, this one was crowded with people. The great majority of them were huddled together in a large group before a house diagonally across the street from the darkened façade of Ford's Theatre. Occasionally, one or more of the silent spectators would drift away from the crowd. One such was an old woman who stepped unwittingly in front of Steele's horse as he urged the animal forward. She looked at the rider, showing no emotion at almost being trampled. Deep shock dwelled behind her moist eyes.

"What's happening here, ma'am?" Steele asked, his voice smoothed by a Virginia drawl as he touched his hat brim with a gloved hand.

The old woman blinked, and a tear was squeezed from the corner of each eye. "Mr. Lincoln," she replied tremulously. "They've shot Mr. Lincoln."

Under different circumstances, Steele knew he might have felt a surge of joy and expectation that the event could signal new hope for the South to rise against defeat. But he had come to Washington determined to forget the past and adjust himself to the best future he could make. Even so, he had difficulty in injecting a degree of the mournful into his voice as he asked, "Is the President dead?"

The old woman shook her head. "He's dying. Won't last out the night, they say."

Steele took a final look down the street, then jerked over the reins to angle his horse toward Elmer's Barroom. It was not in complete darkness, for a dim light flickered far back in one of the windows. After he had looped the reins over the hitching rail at the edge of the sidewalk, he approached the doors and they swung open in front of him.

"We're closed, mister," Elmer announced as the newcomer crossed the threshold. "Mark of respect for the President."

The doors squeaked closed behind Steele and he halted abruptly. He saw Elmer standing behind the bar, using the turned-down light of a single kerosene lamp to count the night's takings. "I just heard," he said, moving toward the bar. "After getting news like that, a man needs a drink. Whiskey."

He pulled up short again as something brushed against his shoulder. As he looked up, he could see the limply hanging form of a dead man. The body revolved slowly from where he had collided with a dangling leg. "Turn up the lamp, bartender," he said softly.

Elmer continued to chink loose change, taking it from his apron pocket and stacking it on the bartop. "Told you, mister, the place is closed up for the night," he growled.

"You don't turn up that lamp, I'll kill you," Steele said, his drawling voice still pitched low. But it was high on menace.

Elmer's head snapped up and he peered intently through the darkness toward the newcomer. He could not see Steele clearly and it was for this reason he reached out and turned up the wick. His free hand dragged a Manhattan Navy Model out from beneath the bar. When the pool of light had spread far enough to illuminate Steele and the hanging man, the revolver was cocked and aimed. "You don't look capable, mister," Elmer said, noting that Steele wore no gunbelt and his hands were empty.

Steele was staring up at the swollen face of the old man. His own features were empty of expression and when he turned to look at Elmer and started to walk toward him he still gave no outward sign of what he was thinking. "What happened here?" he asked, the threat missing from his low tones. But neither was he concerned with the pointing gun in the bartender's hands. He glanced casually to his right and saw a bearded old timer with a bloody forehead climbing painfully to his feet. Then to the left, where a sleeping drunk was just a lumpy shadow against a deeper shadow beneath the table.

Elmer's sullen eyes met Steele's open stare, then took in at close range the man's easy-going features and unprovoking build. He lumped all this together with the lack of visible weapons and decided his unwanted customer had a tough mouth but nothing with which to back it up. He put the gun down beneath the bar and started to dig for more coins. "A guy blasted the President over at the theatre," he rasped. "Got clean away." He nodded toward the man hanging from the beam. "That guy passed the gun to the murderer. Didn't have the sense to take it on the lam." A sour grin twisted his mouth. "Me and a few others kinda forced him to hang around."

The old timer was leaning his elbows on the bar, nursing his broken head in the palms of his hands. "Weren't no proof of that!" he snapped, without looking up. "Ed Binns and his pals just up and hanged the old man on account of what you told 'em."

Elmer glowered hatefully at the old timer. "He give the gun to Booth, I'm telling you," he snarled.

"And you can give me a drink," Steele said.

Elmer sighed, seemed about to refuse, then swung around and swept a shot glass and bottle from the shelf behind him. He set the glass on the bartop and poured the right measure without looking.

Steele proffered no money, and neither did he reach for the drink. "What if you were wrong?" he asked.

Elmer banged the bottle down angrily. "Just drink your drink and get out so I can close up," he ordered. "I weren't wrong."

"You were wrong," Steele said. With his left hand, Steele tugged at his ear lobe. His right hand came fast out of the pocket on that side of the jacket and Elmer's eyes widened with terror as he saw the tiny two-shot derringer clutched in the fist. The gun went off with a small crack. The shattered whiskey bottle made a louder noise. Elmer fell backward, crashing against the display shelf. His hands clutched at his bulbous stomach. Small shards of broken glass glittered against the dark stains of whiskey covering his apron. He looked down at himself and gasped when he saw the blood oozing between his fingers.

"His name was Benjamin Steele. And my name is Adam Steele," the man said softly. "That was my father you killed."

The pain had had time to reach Elmer now, and it overflowed his eyes in the form of tears as he brought his head up to look at the man he had so badly misjudged. Steele held the shocked stare of the other, as he slid the derringer back into his pocket and used his left hand to draw out a match. He struck it on his thumbnail and in the sudden flare of yellow light his eyes seemed not to be as one with the rest of his features. For the lines of his face had a composed, innocuous set—while the eyes, pulled wide, blazed with a seemingly unquenchable fury.

Then the flaring match was arced forward. Elmer emitted a strangled sob of horror, throwing up his hands. The match sailed between them and bounced against his chest. It fell to the floor, but not before a fragile flame licked up from the whiskey-sodden material of his shirt. He beat at it with a blood-stained hand, the motion fanning the fire. Within a terrifying few seconds, as the fury died within Steele, the bartender's massive body was enveloped in searing flames. As shreds of charred clothing fell from him and the intense heat swept over his naked skin, his sobs became strangled cries. He threw himself to the floor and began to roll backward and forward as he beat at the hungry flames. But the whiskey-soaked sawdust only added fuel to the agonizing fire.

The old timer's horror at the lynching was nothing compared to the revulsion he felt as he watched Elmer's pitifully ineffectual attempts to beat out the flames. But he made no effort to intervene, conscious of the evil lurking beneath the deceptively gentle surface of the young man standing beside him.

"Innocent man getting lynched," Steele said, still softly. "Fair burns a man up, doesn't it?"

* * *

The hole was almost as deep as Adam Steele was tall. Reverently he lowered the stiff body of the old man into the bare earth, not looking down into the trench until the corpse was completely covered. Then he worked furiously to shovel the rest of the dirt onto the grave. His fury grew as he realized he wouldn't be able to place a marker on the site.

He gazed once again at the still-smoking ruins of the Steele home. Only a few items were worth salvaging. Souvenirs of better, peaceful days. But Adam would only take one reminder. An unusual weapon, a Colt Hartford sporting rifle, six-shot revolving percussion, .44 caliber, given to his father by the President. The barrel was covered with soot, and the rosewood stock was slightly charred, but the action worked smoothly.

Now Lincoln and Ben Steele were both dead. Two fine lives extinguished by madness . . . two burials marked the beginning of an unending and blood-soaked vengeance trail for Adam Steele.